'I'm afraid I can't marry you, because I shall never marry again.'

There, it was said! And if Dacre was anywhere near as kind as she thought him he would let her return to her room without further argument. But then it was that she discovered that Dacre wasn't so kind as she had believed and that he *did* want a further explanation!

'It's not—just me?' he enquired quietly.

Dear God, she loved him! If anyone, it would be him. 'No,' she answered.

'Then why, Josy,' he wanted to know, 'do you think you will never marry again?'

Dear Reader

If you enjoyed Belvia's story, HEARTLESS PURSUIT by Jessica Steele, published in September last year, you'll love Josy's story in the exciting sequel A WIFE IN WAITING!

Belvia and Josy Fereday were twins. Although they looked alike they were chalk and cheese when it came to their characters. Josy had always been painfully shy whilst Belvia—well, she wasn't afraid of speaking her mind. But when sisters are in a tight spot they stick together!

Now Belvia is happily married Josy realises that she is going to have to put her disastrous marriage behind her and stand on her own two feet. Luckily Dacre Banchereau is there to help her.

The Editor

Jessica Steele lives in a friendly Worcestershire village with her super husband, Peter. They are owned by a gorgeous Staffordshire bull terrier called Daisy, who thinks she's human—they don't like to tell her otherwise. It was Peter who first prompted Jessica to try writing and, after the first rejection, encouraged her to keep on trying. Luckily, with Uruguay the exception, she has so far managed to research inside all the countries in which she has set her books. Her thanks go to Peter for his help and encouragement.

Recent titles by the same author:

HEARTLESS PURSUIT
THE MARRIAGE BUSINESS

A WIFE
IN WAITING

BY
JESSICA STEELE

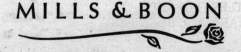

MILLS & BOON

*MILLS & BOON and the Rose Device
are trademarks of the publisher.
Harlequin Mills & Boon Limited,
Eton House, 18-24 Paradise Road, Richmond, Surrey TW9 1SR*

© Jessica Steele 1996

ISBN 0 263 79438 5

*Set in Times Roman 10 on 12 pt.
01-9604-56585 C1*

Made and printed in Great Britain

CHAPTER ONE

JOSY looked through a window of the cross-channel ferry and let go a shaky sigh. Albeit that she would be back from France by Christmas, she had made the break, had made that decision to leave the home she had shared with her father and, hopefully, to start a new kind of life.

Although she had to admit that she felt extremely nervous about what lay in front of her, Josy could not help but be pleased that she had made the decision she had—long delayed though that decison had been. In fact so delayed that it was still a wonder to her that Dacre Banchereau had waited all this while. Particulary since she had agreed to take the job for only six months. She realised she had the family connection to thank for that.

Abruptly she switched her thoughts away from that family connection, and mused instead on how few were the decisions she had ever had to make. She reckoned she could count them on the fingers of one hand.

Her first decision, though panicky, had been to stay home and keep house for her widowed father when she had left school. Some years later she and her twin, Belvia, had reached twenty-one and had come into an inheritance from their much loved mother who had died when they were sixteen.

Josy had bought a car, and decided also to purchase a horse. Dear, dear Hetty—it had been a wrench leaving her, but the next six months would go quickly, and Tracey up at the commercially run stables where Hetty was permanently housed had promised to look after her as if she were her own, and Josy knew she could trust her.

Her lovely brown eyes clouded over as thoughts of the stables inevitably triggered off other memories—memories she did not wish to dwell on but memories which she could not always turn her mind from, memories that returned so constantly to crucify her.

It had been up at the stables where she had met Marc, a shy, unassuming Frenchman. Marc had worked there. She had met him—and had made the biggest decision of all. Last year in early June she had married him.

She choked down a knot of emotion. They had gone to his parents in a village some miles from Nantes for their honeymoon—but before they had been married twenty-four hours Marc was dead. He had been killed in a riding accident and had been dead over ten months now—eleven in two weeks' time—and still she was haunted by her own inadequacies.

She tried not to think about it, to concentrate on this new life she had determined that she must make for herself. She knew that she would never marry again, yet at twenty-three she felt that she had to get out and start to do something with her life. She did not want to go on being her father's housekeeper. And, after the despicable way he had used her—but more outrageously her sister Belvia—for his own devious ends, Josy felt she owed him nothing.

It was partly for Belvia too that she had decided to leave England for a while—Belvia, who had been so wonderfully good to her. This was Belvia's first year of marriage, and to Josy's mind her sister more than deserved that she did not have to worry about her. It was important to Josy that her twin had this time with Latham, her husband, completely worry-free.

Dacre Banchereau, Marc's cousin, a banker whom she had met only once, had been in England on business at the end of September and had made a courtesy call on her. Whereas her French was the schoolgirl variety, and all but forgotten through lack of use, Dacre had spoken English with barely a trace of an accent. And, when all her life she had been plagued by a most disabling and unwanted shyness, she had somehow found Dacre far easier to talk to than most other strangers she'd met.

It could have been, of course, that because he had been a guest in her home she had felt honour-bound to make something of an effort—good manners pushing her to invite him in and offer him refreshment.

All her inhibitions had been out in full force, however, when, glancing at her over the rim of his coffee-cup, he had enquired kindly, 'You are well, Josy?'

She did not like to have anyone's personal attention on her. 'Yes, of course,' she'd replied stiffly.

But, before she had been able to think up anything to say that would take his by now steady scrutiny from her, he'd replaced his cup in his saucer and remarked, 'You are very pale—do you get out in the air?'

'There's the garden. The shopping. The—the . . .' Her voice faded.

'You still have your horse at the stables,' he put in quietly, when she seemed totally stuck for words.

'Hetty. Yes,' she replied stiltedly.

'You manage to ride her every day?'

She did not want him questioning her; she wanted him to go. But he was a guest, was Marc's cousin and, though he was ten years older than her husband's twenty-five years, she knew from her conversations with Marc that there had been a bond between the two as of brothers.

'No,' she replied.

'Every other day?' Dacre suggested.

'No,' she replied again. And, to save him asking, Every week, every other week? went on, 'I haven't ridden at all since I came back—fr-from France, I mean.'

There followed a quite lengthy pause, and again she wanted the tall, good-looking Frenchman gone. But all at once, as she watched, she would have sworn that he lost some of his colour. There was certainly a trace of shock in his voice anyway when abruptly, bluntly, he questioned harshly, 'You are with child?'

'*No*! *No*!' she denied sharply, crimson colour staining her previously pale cheeks. 'I . . .' She turned her head from him, anguish again crucifying her. 'No,' she said once more, her voice a mere whisper this time. Oh, how she wished that she *was* with child—that she *was* pregnant. Oh, if only that were so then she would be rid forever of this torment of guilt at the fact that she had been unable to give herself to Marc.

'Forgive me; please don't be distressed!'

Josy came away from the torture of her memories to see that Dacre no longer appeared shocked, but was looking truly regretful that he had upset her.

'It—w-was a natural assumption, I suppose,' she managed to reply, her good manners holding up when what she wanted to do was to dash from the room rather than stay in what she felt was a strained atmosphere.

She flicked a nervous glance to the watching, observing, grey-eyed man. He seemed to be missing not a thing. Then suddenly, as she looked at him, he smiled a smile of such charm and ease that she stared at him in fascination and all at once forgot to feel strained.

'But you still like horses?' he commented in friendly fashion, swiftly changing the subject back to horses.

'Oh, yes, I love them.' She smiled shyly back, once more finding him easier than most to talk with. Then she saw a light of something almost speculative come into his eyes. It worried her a little.

But his expression was relaxed when unhurriedly he questioned, 'I wonder—and I hope you won't mind my asking—if you could help me?'

'Help you?' she queried. 'How?'

'It's to do with a couple of horses I own,' Dacre replied. 'I live in a very isolated area in the Loire valley—'

'You don't live in Nantes near your aunt and uncle?' she questioned impulsively—Dacre Banchereau had been there at the airport to meet their plane—she had assumed that he lived close by.

'My weekend home is a couple of hours' drive from Nantes, in a place near Saumur. During the week I live and work in Paris.'

'But—you were visiting Marc's parents the day Marc and I . . .' Her voice dried up. Oh, Marc, Marc, Marc. She should never have married him. If they hadn't married they wouldn't have gone to France, and he—

'I was at my weekend home on the day my aunt Sylvie and uncle Philippe received an early morning call from Marc, during which he told them he was coming home that day and bringing someone very special with him,' Dacre revealed, his look alert to the changing, shadowed expressions on her face. 'My aunt in particular was extremely excited. She had the strongest feeling that she was about to meet her future daughter-in-law.'

Josy had known about Marc's phone call, but not the rest of it, and while part of her did not want to hear any more there was another part of her that seemed to need to know more. She'd had plenty of time to think since Marc's death, and only now did she realise that, with Marc having loved horses even more than she did, horses had seemed to be their sole topic of conversation.

'Marc's mother rang you?' she asked.

'She had already phoned my mother, who, during the course of the conversation, said I was not in Paris but at home clearing up a few matters prior to starting a two-week vacation the next day. As soon as Aunt Sylvie had finished that call she rang me, insisting nothing would do but—because I was going away and would miss you and Marc—that I drive over to meet the woman who she was sure was her son's fiancée.' Dacre looked steadily at her for a long, long moment, and then commented, 'The surprise to all of us was that you were already his wife.'

'We didn't mean to hurt anyone!' Josy blurted out in an unhappy rush. 'Neither Marc nor I wanted a big wedding and—'

'My dear, you didn't hurt anyone,' he cut in to soothe understandingly. 'We who are of Marc's family knew of his preference for horses rather than human beings. When we met you we saw that Marc had been exceedingly lucky in that he had found someone with the same reserved temperament as himself.'

Lucky! How could Marc have been lucky? He had married her—and died. 'I...' she began, but felt choked suddenly and could not go on.

She fought desperately hard to get herself back together again, not to break down in front of this man who, for all he was of Marc's family, was a stranger, and as Dacre waited silently, watchfully and patiently she was grateful to him that, observing her emotional state, he gave her the time she needed in which to regain her control.

Then it was that he gave her something else to think about when he continued, 'To go back to the great help you could be to me. I live in a very isolated location, as I mentioned and, since I need someone to look after my horses, and with you loving horses so much—' He broke off. Then, looking at her with a steady grey gaze, he asked, 'I don't suppose you'd be interested in the job?'

'No!' she replied before he could draw another breath.

'It would be too isolated for you?'

'It isn't that,' Josy answered, and, realising that her manners had slipped and that her refusal had been too blunt, went on, 'I think I should like very much to live in an isolated area, but...'

'But you've no wish to live in France?'

It wasn't even that. 'I th-think I might like to live in France,' she told him honestly, and, starting to feel a mite panicky, added, 'But I couldn't come—I keep house for my father. He—'

'You're entitled to a life of your own, Josy,' he interrupted, and there was that something not to be put off in his tone that disturbed her.

'I know,' she replied, only just holding down her panic. 'But—but—I told you, I don't ride now. I've had nothing to do with horses since Marc died.'

For long, long moments after these words had left her Dacre Banchereau just sat silently looking at her. And then very quietly he let fall, 'Don't you think that you should?' She opened her mouth to say no, but, still talking quietly, he went on to state that just because Marc had died while out riding he would not have wanted her to deny herself the sport of riding which they had both loved, ending, 'And, talking of horses, are you now going to show me the stables where my cousin worked?'

'Stables?' she gasped, oblivious of his level-eyed gaze. She had avoided the stables like the plague since she had returned from France almost four months ago. 'I—I—I don't go to the stables! I haven't been to the stables since I got back!' she stated agitatedly.

'Then I think,' Dacre replied calmly, 'that it's time that you did.'

Josy stared at him, to her astonishment feeling quite angry with him. She, who seldom ever felt anything so positive as anger, realised that she felt astonishingly angry with him and his interference.

'I...' she began defiantly, and saw his grey glance go to the angry sparks flashing in her eyes—as if her anger surprised him as much as it did her. And as she remembered some of her own recent thoughts and feelings on the subject of the stables—only just lately she had started to wonder herself if she should try and do the self-same thing that he was suggesting—suddenly her anger fizzled out. Her sister had been little short of an angel—exercising Hetty every day for her, loving, protecting and caring for her. But many had been the times over the last week or two when Josy had thought that she wasn't being fair to Belvia—that she really should make an effort. 'D-do you really want to—to see where Marc worked?' she heard herself ask.

Dacre's firm gaze held hers. She then saw that steady look move over her pale, unblemished complexion, rest on her long fair hair with its hint of red, before it came back to her large, deeply brown eyes. 'Yes,' he said, looking straight into them. 'I really do.'

Josy clenched her hands tightly as she fought to find the courage she would need. She owed it to her dear twin, who had done so much for her, to be strong. She owed it to Marc—oh, my heavens, how she owed it to

Marc. And because of Marc, whose family had lost him, she owed it very much to this man Dacre Banchereau, who had loved him more as a younger brother than a cousin, to be strong and to do as he asked and show him where Marc had worked and been happy.

'C-could you—would you w-wait while I go and get changed?' she asked.

'Of course,' he replied kindly.

Josy left the room, but when she returned she had changed not from her everyday dress into a smarter outfit but—and it had taken all of her courage to do it—was wearing her riding clothes.

Dacre was on his feet. 'R-ready?' Josy asked jerkily, saw his glance flick over the long length of her legs in their well-fitting jodhpurs and had her answer when he joined her at the door.

They went to the stables in his car, and Josy silently owned to feeling all strung up and tense when, leaving him to follow, she went looking for Hetty. But the moment she saw her so, for the first time in almost four months, Josy felt something in her start to come back to life.

'Oh, Hetty, Hetty,' she crooned, the fact that Dacre Banchereau was but a yard or so behind her entirely lost to her as warmth for the horse flooded her heart. She hugged Hetty and laid her face against her neck, and Hetty whinnied in approval.

How long she stood there stroking the mare, a glow of loving about her, life entering her being, Josy did not know. But, her eyes still alight, some slight sound made her turn around, and then it was that she remembered Dacre.

She looked at him, felt shy, but because for the first time in an age she had experienced a small fraction of inner peace she just had to say a quiet, 'Thank you.'

And he understood, it seemed, for he just looked back at her, his eyes travelling over her expressive face. Then softly he hinted, 'It would be a pity not to put those jodhpurs to good use.'

In truth Josy was not at all sure why she had changed into her riding clothes, save that she always dressed like this when she came to the stables. But Hetty looked willing and eager, and as more life lit Josy's eyes so she found that she was asking, 'Will you wait?'

'I will wait,' Dacre confirmed solemnly, and the next she knew was that he was helping her to saddle up.

And wait for her he did, and when, with a hint of pink in her otherwise pale cheeks, Josy returned, he helped her unsaddle Hetty and attend to her before he drove Josy back to her home.

Outside her house she wondered if she should ask him in. But in the close confines of his car she felt shy again, and was not sure that she wanted him inside her home a second time. However, good manners being what they were, she was about to invite him in just the same when he got out of the car, came round and opened the passenger door. And as she got out and stood with him on the pavement for a moment he asked her to, 'Think about my suggestion, Josy. I need someone reliable to look after my horses.'

'I—' she began to decline.

'Think about it,' he urged. 'Think about it most carefully. If you feel you can come for only a short while—say six months—think about it.'

'I...' Again she was about to refuse.

'I'm hardly ever there. Some weekends I don't make it at all,' he informed her. And with a disarming smile added, 'I should feel happy to know that a member of my family was there.'

How nice he made that sound! 'I'll—er—think about it,' she heard herself promise.

And Dacre went away, and she did think about it, right until the next morning when Belvia came home from spending the weekend with a friend. Barely had she told her sister all about Dacre's visit when Latham Tavenner came looking for Bel. And then—staggeringly—Belvia, with an adoring Latham by her side, told her that they were getting married.

Josy gasped at the shock of that and later, when her sister told her all she had to tell her—including what their father had been up to in his endeavours to get Latham to invest in his company—there was no space in which to think about Dacre's suggestion that she go to France to work for him.

Five days later, as September gave way to October— and after a whirlwind of shopping and arranging—Belvia and Latham married. Belvia looked radiant, and Latham looked as if he could not believe that she had not only agreed to marry him but had just said so in church.

And, for Belvia and the love she had for her, Josy managed to overcome her shyness to be her bridesmaid— only Belvia and Latham being aware that because of her married status she was more matron of honour than bridesmaid.

Josy had never told her father that she had married Marc. In fact her father had never met Marc. She had wanted to bring him home one time, but her father was a snob of the first water and had looked down his nose at the idea of her bringing a mere groom into his home.

And Josy had thought too much of Marc to introduce him into such an atmosphere.

She'd no idea then, though, that because he was averse to meeting people Marc had opted for a simple life when in actual fact he came from quite a wealthy background. Only when they had been married and on their honeymoon flight to tell his parents of their marriage had Marc confided about the businesses his father owned, and the fact that he had no need to work at all unless he wanted to.

Her head was still filled with thoughts of Marc, and of Belvia and Latham and their wonderful happiness a week later. She also thought a great deal about her father and his treachery. And then she started to think too of Dacre Banchereau's job offer.

It would mean leaving her father to look after himself, but after the way he had behaved Josy felt little compunction about doing that. She had planned to leave home anyway when she and Marc returned from their honeymoon, though she had planned to look in on her old home daily to check her father's larder and his laundry. But, as Bel had said only a couple of weeks ago, 'Let him pay for a housekeeper.'

Suddenly it all seemed possible—if she dared. For Belvia, and for herself. It would mean leaving Hetty, but she was such a lovable mare that everybody wanted to spoil her—and would. And it would only be for six months—Josy was certain about that as she began to look on Dacre's offer as a lifeline.

She felt she needed to get away, to take stock, to make the break from her domineering father. What better chance? If she went to France there would be no way that he would ring her when he couldn't find something or other and expect her to come home and find it for him.

Some weeks ago she had started to think that she couldn't go on like this, that she must make more of an effort. Whilst still swamped by guilt, she was better than she had been, and over the worst of the shock, at what had happened, which had so rocked her.

Those first few weeks after Marc's death—his funeral, she and Belvia flying home and Belvia covering for her so that their father should know none of it—had passed for the most part in a traumatised haze.

It was only lately that Josy had begun to realise how much she owed her sister. Bel had at once dropped everything to rush to France to be with her, had supported her, and back in England she had defended her, been an avenging angel for her—and Josy knew that she would be forever grateful to her.

But Belvia was married now, and while there would always be a strong bond between them Josy realised that it was time to let go. She took a deep breath and at that moment determined that she would take up Dacre Banchereau's offer.

Then the phone rang, and to her amazement it was him! 'How are you, Josy?' he enquired.

'I'm very well,' she replied politely.

'Can I hope you have made a decision in my favour?' he asked, without further ado.

Josy took a shaky breath, but the determination of her decision a moment ago was still warm, and while her nerve held out, with a 'neck or nothing' kind of gulp, she told him, 'I should like to—um—take the job for six months.' The taut kind of silence that followed was equally unnerving—so much so that Josy found herself blurting out, 'I don't speak much French—well, hardly any at all, really.'

'That's no problem,' Dacre's voice came back charmingly in her ears. 'Would you like me to come for you?'

'Oh, no.' She at once rejected the idea. 'I can come by myself.'

'When?' he wanted to know, now that he had her acceptance of the job seeming to be impatient for her to start.

'I don't—er—can I let you know? I—um—haven't told my father yet.'

'You won't let him change your mind?'

'No, I won't do that,' she promised, and heard Dacre all businesslike as he asked her if she had a pen and gave her his telephone numbers where she could contact him.

In the event, however, over six months were to pass before Josy was able to keep her promise and leave England for France. To start with, her father was not at all pleased to hear that the streamlined running of his existence was going to be interfered with.

'I don't want to employ a housekeeper,' he snapped angrily.

Josy looked at him and thought of the many times she had given in to his likes and dislikes. She thought of the dreadful life he had given her mother. And she thought of his deviousness and—for only the second time in her life—she stood up to him. 'The house is going to get very untidy without one,' she told him.

'Did your sister put you up to this?' he snarled.

'Belvia's still away on her honeymoon,' she reminded him.

'You're horse-mad!' he attacked nastily—and the next day went down with a heavy bout of flu.

Josy rang Dacre. 'I'm sorry, my father's ill with flu. I don't know when I'll be able to come.'

'You've told him you're coming to France?'

'Yes—but... If you don't want to wait... I mean, it's only a temporary job, after all. If you want to get somebody else...' she offered, seeing her chance of going getting away from her.

'You're family—I'll wait,' Dacre replied.

Never had she known flu to last so long. She was still nursing her father well into November. 'Don't you think you should try to go into work?' she dared to hint.

'Latham Tavenner's had the nerve to send his accountants in!'

'That's natural enough, surely, since he intends to invest a tremendous sum in your company?' Josy suggested fairly.

'Well, they can do it without getting any answers from me!' he declared spitefully. 'If they ring tell them I'm indisposed.'

Josy rang Dacre Banchereau again in December. 'I should still like to come, but I don't feel I can leave my father alone over Christmas and New Year,' she stated.

'I'll see you in January,' he clipped, sounding not at all pleased, and put the phone down.

Only then, as she began to panic that the job was going away from her, did Josy realise that she really wanted this chance to change her life. Much to her relief, however, Dacre rang her on Christmas Day and seemed much more friendly.

'I wanted to wish you the best Christmas you can have,' he stated, and Josy started to feel quite warm towards him, knowing that he must have been thinking of Marc and realising that she must be feeling particularly low at being without him at this festive time.

She didn't want his sympathy, though. She was still weighed down by guilt—and didn't want to think about it. 'Thank you,' she replied. 'Have a good Christmas.' She had nothing more to add, so rang off—and oddly found that she was wondering in which of his two homes he was spending Christmas—and who with. He was a good-looking, virile, sophisticated man—it went without saying that he would not be spending it alone.

At one time such a man would have terrified her. But Belvia and Latham—sometimes with Latham's own sister, sometimes not—frequently urged her to dine with them, and the more she got to know her sophisticated and worldly-wise brother-in-law, the more she began to feel less constrained and more comfortable in a sophisticated man's company.

She made another call to Dacre in January, to tell him that she was having trouble finding a suitable housekeeper for her father.

'Please feel free to forget about your job offer if you feel I'm messing you about,' she ended, and prayed hard that his feelings about her being family would hold up—because by then, while still nervous to some extent, she had started to feel quite excited at the prospect of going to Dacre's home.

'You insult my French honour,' he replied—and she realised that he was teasing.

'Er—g-goodbye,' she said, and fancied that she liked his teasing.

It was in February that her sister took a hand in interviewing the next set of potential employees and decided that a stern-eyed Mrs Vale was ideal for the job of keeping house for their ill-humoured father.

'Mrs Vale has to give notice to her present employer,' Belvia said when they had seen her out. 'So I've arranged for her to start on the first of April.'

'Father will want to see her to give the OK first,' Josy told her lovely blonde-haired sister.

'Tough!' Belvia laughed. To Josy's mind she seemed to have grown more beautiful than ever since her marriage. 'I've told Mrs Vale that her salary will be paid monthly into her bank, and I'll arrange that since the old skinflint is likely to use "Can't afford it" as another excuse. Now, you just get on that phone to France. You still want to go, love?'

Josy nodded, and because she thought it only fair to Mrs Vale to stay with her for a couple of weeks she decided to give Dacre a date in the middle of April.

'And that's definite?' Dacre asked.

'Most definitely definite,' she replied, and laughed— and when there was a short silence on the other end realised that to hear her laugh must have surprised him as much as it had surprised her. She had laughed little lately. 'I—um—I'll make my own way,' she added quickly. 'Is there anyone I should see if you're not home that weekend?'

'I'll make a point of being there. And I'll also send you directions,' he answered, which she thought was very nice, and then, before he rang off, he added, 'Nina and César are looking forward to seeing you.'

'Nina and César?'

'Your charges,' Dacre informed her.

'Ah—um—it's all right that I'm taking the job for only six months?' she thought to ask, after all this while still anxious at the last minute.

'Perfectly all right,' he answered evenly, and, with nothing more to be discussed between them, bade her, '*Au revoir*.'

True to his word, directions for how to get to Saumur, and very detailed directions for how to get from there to his home, arrived—and Josy started packing.

She had decided to travel on a Friday, to stay overnight in Normandy, and to drive on to Saumur and from there to Dacre's home the following morning.

It was, perhaps, with the view that her father might be unpleasant to her on her last night home that Belvia and Latham invited themselves to dinner on Thursday evening.

'You've nothing to worry about, I feel sure,' Belvia told her confidently as they were leaving. 'I haven't met Dacre Banchereau, it's true, but his parents were at Marc's funeral and they seemed lovely people.'

Josy couldn't remember them. But that was not surprising. Apart from the fact that many, many other people had been there to pay their respects, she had been in deep shock, and little else had registered but that Marc was dead and wouldn't have been if...

Belvia hugged her tightly. 'I'll miss you.' She smiled—her eyes shiny.

Latham put an arm around his wife's shoulders and held her close to him as he in turn smiled at his sister-in-law and told her, 'Remember, Jo, any problems and we can be with you within hours.'

'I'll remember,' she smiled, but did not anticipate any problems, and said goodbye to them realising that Belvia had been right when ages ago—when Josy had started to surface from her shock about Marc—she had said that her uncertainty about everything would pass. Because never would she have thought that she would so much as contemplate the step she was taking now—not only leaving home and taking a job, but a job in a foreign country!

An announcement to car drivers over the cross-channel ferry's speaker system brought Josy out of her reverie. People started to move—they had arrived in France!

She had never driven on what she thought of as the wrong side of the road before, but after her first fifteen minutes of intense concentration she discovered that there was nothing to it. She had never had any problems with driving and, while confidence had never been her strong suit, she drove with confidence and care.

Josy found the hotel she had a reservation with—one Latham's PA had arranged for her—and went up to her room, feeling she would like to phone Dacre to say that she had arrived in his country.

Shyness and a feeling that since she would be seeing him tomorrow he would probably think her an idiot held her back. She had a meal sent to her room, and went to bed.

Josy was an early riser, and was up and on her way by eight on Saturday morning. This was it; this was the start of her new life. She had made the break from home, from her father. She would see how things went, and when she returned to England—if her nerve held out— she would see about finding somewhere else to live, see about finding another job.

The remainder of the money her mother had left her was still substantial but it wouldn't last for ever. She might find a live-in job looking after horses. She'd like that. She might even be able to have Hetty with her. She'd *have* to have Hetty with her, she decided with un- usual determination. It sounded a bit grand but she would truthfully be able to tell any prospective employer that her last job had been looking after a stables in France.

Josy smiled at her temerity. Grief, she hadn't started the job yet—and Dacre had only two horses. But they were stables, weren't they? She decided there and then that she was going to be more positive.

Feeling more light-hearted than she had in an age, she motored on. When she came to the sizeable town of Angers, however, some of her new-found confidence took a dip. Saumur and surrounds, she calculated, were getting on for an hour's drive away.

She had no idea what time they had lunch in Dacre's household, but she did not want to arrive slap bang in the middle of it. And even though it was over six months since she had seen Dacre Banchereau she remembered him clearly—dark-haired, grey-eyed, tall, good-looking, mid-thirties and sophisticated with it . . . and, to be painfully honest, she was starting to feel overwhelmingly shy again.

Josy left her car in a cark park in Angers and took a stroll around town. She also, and not without taking a deep breath, entered a café and ordered what she thought was a sandwich, but—her French being as poor as she had supposed—it turned out to be half a French loaf stuffed with everything one could imagine.

She was too embarrassed to leave it—yet didn't know how to start it. Then suddenly she started to get cross with herself. This was her new life. She was a new person. Two-handedly she raised the filled French bread to her mouth and began her chewing marathon.

She arrived in Saumur some time after half-past two. At three-fifteen, Dacre's directions having been faultless, she pulled up outside his house. Though 'house', she

rather thought, was a misnomer. For, endorsing her
knowledge that Marc came from moneyed people, in her
view it was more of a manor-house. It stood in its own
grounds with parkland about and not another dwelling
in sight.

She loved its splendid isolation and, wondering if she
had after all made a mistake with the directions, she got
out of her car with Dacre's instructions in her hand.
Taking her glance from the white-fronted, many-
windowed, two-storeyed building, she looked from the
wide expanse of drive over extensive lawns with a small
wood beyond, and then checked his directions again.

Then she discovered that she had not made a mistake,
and nor did she need to check the paper in her hand,
for a voice called, 'Josy!' She looked up at the sound
of her name, and relief flooded through her.

'Dacre,' she answered, shyness taking her as the tall
Frenchman, clad in trousers, shirt and light sweater, came
from the house and over the gravel drive to greet her.

Her instinctive good manners pushed their way
through her shyness, and as he reached her she extended
a dainty hand to him—and then she realised that she
was well and truly in France, when, ignoring her out-
stretched hand, Dacre extended both his hands to her.
'Welcome to my home.' He smiled, his grey eyes taking
in her hair, her face and her person, clad similarly in
trousers and light sweater.

Josy felt his hands on her arms, felt him drawing her
closer. She tried hard not to panic, and discovered as he
came yet closer that even for a man with such an athletic
build he had a surprisingly broad chest. Then she felt
his skin against hers as unhurriedly he kissed first one
of her cheeks and then the other.

She felt hot all over. Even while her brain registered that this was the way any Frenchman would greet someone whom he considered to be a member of his family she felt hot and in need of taking in great gulps of air.

She pushed him away, saw her action register with him, and then felt awkward and embarrassed and wanted the ground to open up and swallow her. From somewhere, though—and maybe it stemmed from her earlier decision to be more positive—she managed a smile. And as his hands fell away from her, she stated, 'I'm glad to be here.' And hoped that only she knew just how much the feel of his kisses to her cheeks had disconcerted her.

CHAPTER TWO

'YOU will be tired after your journey. We'll leave your luggage until you've had some refreshment, some lunch...' Dacre went on and, shy or not, Josy just had to interrupt.

'I had lunch in Angers,' she butted in to reveal, then added quickly, rather than cause offence, 'But I'd love a cup of tea.' Oh, grief, she was in France. 'Or coffee,' she as quickly tacked on.

'We drink tea in France, too,' he teased, his eyes alight on her worried look. 'I'm sure my housekeeper has the kettle already boiling.'

Josy walked over the gravel drive with him and she started to feel more relaxed—his teasing was responsible, she guessed.

'Your journey was without mishap?' he enquired conversationally as they went through the stout front door and into an elegant hall that had a beautiful mahogany staircase that seemed to go on for ever, and divided at the top to form a crescent-shaped landing.

'Yes, thank you,' she replied politely, and walked alongside him past various closed doors until they came to one which was open and which was clearly the drawing-room door. No doubt Dacre had been taking his ease in this room when he had heard and possibly seen her car arrive.

Before they could enter the room, however, a neatly clad lady somewhere in her middle fifties appeared from around the corner of the long hall. Dacre, with a mur-

mured 'My housekeeper' for Josy's benefit, waited for
her to approach and introduced her.

Josy was normally reserved in her greetings, but as
Agathe Audoin went a tinge pink, and as Josy recognised in the housekeeper a shyness which she herself had
always endured, it triggered in her a need to put a fellow
sufferer at ease.

'*Comment allez-vous, madame*?' she dredged up a
half-forgotten French 'How are you?' and even found
a smile to go with it as she stretched out a hand to the
housekeeper.

The housekeeper's reply was to smile, shake hands and
reply with a brief something in very fast French which
was totally incomprehensible to Josy. But as Josy turned
to glance at Dacre she saw that he was looking at her as
if arrested by something.

Before she could start to feel anxious about what that
something might be, though, he was giving Agathe some
instructions and, with a start, Josy definitely picked up
the words Madame Paumier—her own married name.

Agathe went on her way, and Dacre ushered Josy into
the superb, high-ceilinged drawing-room. It was exquis-
itely furnished with lush carpets and French antique
furniture.

'Agathe will not be many minutes with your tea,' he
commented, while at the same time indicating that she
should take a seat in one of the lovely high-backed chairs.

But as she went over to one of them and sat down,
and realised that he had just given Agathe instructions
about some refreshments, she realised too that Dacre
Banchereau was not a man to pretend that he had not
noticed something when he had. For no sooner had he
taken a seat opposite her, than, looking at her, he was

remarking, 'You seemed surprised, Josy, that I should refer to you as Madame Paumier?'

There was a question there, and Josy half wished that she hadn't come. Then she caught herself up short. Good grief! Was this the way to make a fresh life—to want to bolt at the first minor hurdle? To want to run for cover the moment someone said something that touched a raw nerve? Dacre wasn't to know of her guilt, nor of the fact that she had never felt married.

'I...' she tried. There had definitely been a question in his voice. She didn't know how to answer.

'Forgive me—perhaps I'm being insensitive,' he apologised, when he could see she was stuck for words. 'You're not wearing your wedding ring, I know, but—' he broke off, and, insensitive or not, enquired, 'Is it that you prefer to be known as Miss Fereday?'

'Er...' She was sorely tempted to grab at that suggestion. But suddenly, as she looked at him, she checked, halted when the words were on her lips to say that, Yes, that was it—that in this emancipated world she preferred to be known by her single name. Somehow, as she looked at him, looked into those steady grey eyes, she felt that she could not lie to him. He made her feel that she would be letting herself down if she did. She swallowed. He shouldn't be able to do that to her. He was nothing to her but a cousin-in-law—if there was such a thing—and yet he gave her a feeling that if she was going to make any kind of a life for herself then she wasn't going to make much of a start on it by being dishonest. Somehow she was going to have to be both brave and honest—and Dacre's steady gaze seemed to refuse to allow her to be anything less. 'It—isn't that,' she replied, realising that he was patiently waiting for her to answer. 'I—just—er—don't feel as if I've ever been married.'

'Oh—poor Josy. I'm so sorry. I didn't mean to cause you pain,' he at once apologised. 'You were married for less than a day and—'

'Please don't sympathise,' she interrupted. It wasn't right—she had no right to his sympathy. She took a shaky breath. 'I . . .' she began, with no clear idea of what she was going to say.

But, as if realising that to talk of her brief marriage was upsetting her, Dacre stated soothingly, 'Marc would have been pleased that you came to me.' And she supposed then that he had known Marc far better than she had.

'You must miss him,' she in turn sympathised.

'There was a ten-year age-difference between us, so naturally I had different pursuits. But our mothers are sisters; we shared the same blood and were close—' He broke off at the sound of a trolley being wheeled along the hall. 'Your tea, I think,' he murmured, and went to open the door for Agathe.

He spent a few seconds in conversation with his housekeeper before turning his attention back to his latest employee to ask, 'Have you your car keys, Josy? Franck, Agathe's husband, will take your cases to your room.'

Josy wanted to protest that she could do it. She had after all brought her luggage from her room at home and loaded up her car without help—her father having been in a sulk. Not that he'd have done it anyway. But Dacre obviously employed Franck to do that sort of thing, and she had no wish to tread on anyone's toes. She handed over her car keys.

'Are you having tea too?' she asked of Dacre, when Agathe plus car keys had gone and everything from the trolley was laid out in front of her on a low table.

'*Certainement*,' he accepted.

She picked up a most delicate china cup and saucer, sent up a prayer that she wouldn't spill it or, even worse, drop it, and poured out some tea. 'Milk?' she enquired.

'Why not?' he replied, and she realised that she quite liked this tea-drinking, milk-taking man, who was doing his best to make her feel at home. Miraculously she poured and delivered his tea without mishap. 'I can recommend my housekeeper's pastries,' he suggested, offering her an appetising plate of cakes.

'I'm still full from lunch,' she refused, and, remembering the gargantuan repast she had struggled with in Angers, thought it possible that she would still be full up come dinnertime.

She glanced from him to one of the three long windows from where she could see parkland and woods. 'It's idyllic here,' she murmured. Already the peace and tranquillity of the place where Dacre had his home were getting to her.

'You don't think it will be too quiet for you?'

She turned to look at him, and saw that he was serious. 'Never,' she replied quietly. 'I wonder you can ever leave here.'

'Paris has its attractions too,' he replied, and suddenly, as she wondered if he had a steady girlfriend in Paris, another thought struck her. 'You're not married, are you?' she asked, and all at once went a shade of pink. 'I'm sorry; I'm being personal.'

'Josy, my dear, you're part of my family,' Dacre answered straight away, seeing her embarrassment born of shyness. 'I should like very much for us to know each other better. So, please, you must ask anything you wish to know.'

She stared at him with direct honest eyes. He had successfuly sent any embarrassment on its way and she thanked him for that. And it was kind of him to say that, because she was part of his family he wanted them to know each other better. But she had always been reluctant with friendships, and didn't quite know how she felt about anyone getting to know her better.

Josy considered him seriously, her expression unsmiling. Then she thought of Marc and remembered how—if she could only wipe away the last twenty-four hours of their knowing each other—he had been her best friend, apart from Belvia. She felt that he would have urged her to be friends with his cousin—to get to know him better and, if she could, let his cousin know her better too.

So she smiled her rare smile. 'And—*are* you married, *monsieur*?' she asked mischievously, owning to feeling slightly staggered to find suddenly that she had an imp of mischief in her.

So too did the Frenchman appear a touch taken aback. But suddenly he smiled that smile that was so charm-filled and which she had seen once before in England. 'I am not married.' He answered her question on the second time of asking. 'Nor am I seriously involved with anyone at the moment.'

'Oh,' Josy mumbled, realising that the attractions in Paris he had spoken of must be its monuments: the Louvre, Notre Dame cathedral, the world-renowned nightclubs—all in direct contrast to his home here.

Then it was that she saw how Dacre had the best of both worlds. Undoubtedly he worked hard, but when his day's work was done there was always the Paris nightlife—and whether 'seriously involved' or not, it was without question that he did not relax alone. And when his week's work was done what better pleasure than to leave the enjoyment of the bustling capital and come home here, to this serene and beautiful place?

Her tea finished, she glanced opposite and saw that he had been studying her. She looked quickly away, to his teacup reposing on the table. He had finished too.

Casually he rose from his chair. 'Would you like to see your room?'

She went with him from the drawing-room and up the thickly carpeted elegant staircase. They reached the landing where there seemed to be an equal number of rooms going to the right as to the left. Dacre led the way to the right.

'I thought you would be comfortable in this room,' he commented when about four doors along he stopped, opened a door, and stood back to allow her to enter.

And that was when Josy knew that she was to be treated as a member of the family and not as an employee. The room she had been given was not the usual kind of stable-girl's room, she was sure, and her breath caught at the beauty of it.

More French antiques, in the shape of wardrobes, chests and a dressing-table, complemented the room. There was a four-poster bed draped in cream velvet with coffee-coloured, hand-embroidered tie-backs, that matched exactly the curtains at the windows. She turned on the ankle-deep cream carpet. 'It's beautiful!' she breathed. 'A lovely room.'

Dacre stared at her rapt expression for some moments. Then very quietly he stated, 'It is my wish that you grow to be happy here.' And as he turned to check on her luggage which had been brought up Josy felt quite touched by his words.

'Thank you,' she murmured, realising that while she was nothing like the mess she had been those first few months after Marc's death she still had quite some way to go before she could be happy, and that Dacre, a more sensitive man than she had recognised, had seen that.

'I shall leave you now to rest. We'll eat at eight, but come down to the *salon* as soon as you wish.'

Again she offered her thanks, but when he had gone she knew that she would not go seeking him out until it was time to take their evening meal.

She would have liked to take a look around outside, to say hello to Nina and César, but—she glanced at her watch and saw with surprise that it was already half-past four—she was reluctant to poach on any more of Dacre's free time.

He was in her mind a good deal of the time as she investigated a door leading off her bedroom. She saw that it was a cream-coloured bathroom with fluffy cream towels with coffee-coloured embroidered hems.

She returned to her bedroom, noticing that she had a splendid view from both of the long windows. She realised uncomfortably then that Dacre was according her every respect because she was his cousin's widow.

All too clearly he had a strong sense of family, and, in his dear cousin's memory, nothing was too good for Marc's widow. Worriedly Josy paced from one window to the other. It wasn't right. She hadn't been a wife to Marc, so how right could it be that she was being housed as such?

She could feel herself starting to get agitated, and in desperate need of something to do she unlatched one of her two suitcases and set to work unpacking.

When at last both of her cases were empty, everything she had brought with her either hung up or folded away, she had worked through her agitation and, since she had determined only that morning to be positive, she had found a plus in the fact that Dacre *needed* her.

He needed someone reliable, someone he could trust to look after his horses. He needed someone who would not be put off by the isolation of his home and, with that special discernment he seemed to have—that sensitivity—he had seen that she would do splendidly.

Starting to feel very much better suddenly, but still shy enough not to want to leave her room before ten to eight, Josy remembered that he had left her so she might rest. She did not feel in the need of a rest, but... She glanced at the phone in her room, thought about ringing Belvia to say that she had safely arrived but made herself resist.

Belvia had a different sort of life now and, although they were so close that they would think of each other often, Josy was determined that her sister should enjoy this first year of her marriage to Latham without having to think and worry about her the whole while.

Having been sidetracked, she thought again of how Dacre had greeted her—'You will be tired after your journey'. Who was she to argue? She found that she was smiling as she slipped off her shoes, rolled back the beautifully embroidered bedcover, climbed on to the double four-poster and lay down.

She had not thought that she was at all sleepy, but the bed was the last word in comfort. Her last waking thought was a scrappy reasoning that with the town of Saumur—with its picturesque château on the banks of the Loire, the longest river in France—not more than half an hour's drive away then the situation where Dacre had his home was nowhere near as isolated as it would have been before motorised transport. She hadn't decided whether she was glad or sorry about that when sleep claimed her.

Josy awoke with a start to see that it was a quarter to seven. Good heavens—and she was a poor sleeper! She yawned delicately, and guessed that there must be something magical in the air around this delightful place. And then she remembered that dinner was at eight o'clock, and for someone who wasn't too fussed about eating, especially after she had eaten enough at lunchtime to last her all day, she was starting to grow hungry—it had to be that magical air again.

She was in the bath prior to getting ready for dinner when she suddenly found that she was pondering what she would wear. Good heavens, it must be that magic again—she could not remember the last time she had worried about what to wear.

At ten to eight she had her long fair hair neatly brushed, the smattering of make-up she wore neatly applied and, having opted for a fine wool dress of a deep apricot shade, she was ready to go down to dinner. Unfortunately, having felt quite hungry at seven-thirty, she now didn't feel hungry at all, and would have much preferred by far to remain in her room until breakfast-time.

At five to eight a mixture of good manners, which decreed unpunctuality to be a sin—especially since Madame Audoin might already have the starter ready to serve—together with impatience with herself and the *un*-positive person who was trying to weaken her made Josy leave her room.

She owned to feeling a need to hold on to the mahogany banister as she made her way down the stairs, and in need of clutching on to it when, perhaps some slight sound having alerted him, Dacre came from the open drawing-room door as she reached the bottom stair.

She was aware of his gaze on her as he moved towards her, and she forced herself to go on.

'Your rest has done you good,' he commented pleasantly.

'I went to sleep.' The words just seemed to slip out. 'I didn't mean to—f-fall asleep, I mean—but—' She broke off, feeling dreadful. Grief, here he was, a sophisticated man, and she was prattling on. She felt gauche, ridiculous—and wanted to go home. She fell silent.

He placed a hand on her elbow, guiding her to the drawing-room. 'Perhaps an aperitif before dinner?' he suggested.

'Oh, no,' she refused straight away. 'Thank you,' she remembered her manners. The idea of sitting—or standing, for that matter—in the drawing-room with Dacre, trying to make small talk as she sipped a pre-dinner drink was destroying.

'You don't drink alcohol?' he enquired, halting at the drawing-room door and, since he still had a light hold on her elbow, causing her to halt too.

Josy looked up into cool grey eyes and felt lost for words suddenly. Then with relief she recalled her earlier thoughts on the subject of punctuality. 'It isn't that. It's—well, I've no wish to be discourteous to you, but I shouldn't like to be rude to Madame Audoin either.' She took her eyes from his to consult her watch. 'It's eight o'clock,' she advised him.

He did not move, not for a second or two, but just looked down at her. Then as a warm light entered his eyes he murmured, 'You're very sweet.' And as he bent his head a little she had the strangest notion that he was about to drop a light kiss on her cheek. Quickly she pulled back but, before she could panic, and to show just how very wrong she had been, he agreed easily, 'We must not keep Agathe waiting,' and escorted her further up the hall. And Josy knew that he would have been amazed if he'd realised how she had misread what must have been no more than a small bow in acknowledgement of her reminder of his housekeeper's efforts in the kitchen.

The dining-room was furnished as superbly as the rest of the rooms she had seen. The dining-table was a long, long affair, but only one end had been laid.

Dacre saw her seated and took his own place, and then his housekeeper was there to serve them a delicious starter of various types of mushrooms that had been marinated in wine and spices.

'This is really good,' Josy could not refrain from commenting, her non-existent appetite suddenly reawakened.

'We grow a lot of mushrooms in this area,' he informed her pleasantly. 'But this particular dish is one I believe Agathe made specially for you, to make you welcome.'

'Oh, how kind,' she responded, and felt truly touched by the housekeeper's thoughtfulness—so much so that when the shy housekeeper came in to clear away their used dishes and to serve the next course, Josy plucked up courage and plunged into, '*Merci, madame, pour bons champignons*.' And, while she felt that her 'Thank you, madam, for the good mushrooms,' was woefully inadequate for such a splendid offering, she saw that the housekeeper, who had replied something which was too fast for her to comprehend, was looking very pleased.

'Agathe has requested that you use her first name,' Dacre informed her as the housekeeper departed.

'Then I shall,' Josy answered, and although she rather thought that any alcohol used in the recipe would have evaporated in the heat of cooking she was at a loss to know why else she should find she was beginning to relax.

She certainly felt more comfortable with Dacre than she would have thought possible half an hour ago, she mused as she took her first sip from the glass of wine he had poured to go with the lamb cutlets in pastry. It could have been because he had been telling her how France's national equestrian centre, the Cadre Noir, was situated locally—anything to do with horses tended to make her forget her inhibitions.

But, whatever it was putting her at her ease—either Dacre or the subject—when he was done she found herself mentioning, 'Will my car be all right where I left it?'

'I have garaged it for you. I will show you around tomorrow morning.'

'Thank you.' She smiled, and looked forward in particular to visiting the stables.

'You have been driving long?' he enquired.

'Since I was twenty-one. I'm sorry, that doesn't answer your question. Two years,' she added, and, having just told him she was twenty-three, continued, 'Belvia, my twin sister, taught me to drive.'

'You're not identical twins?' he asked, explaining, 'I'm sure one of my family would have mentioned it had that been so.'

Her eyes clouded over. His family would have seen her and her twin together at Marc's funeral. 'No, we're not,' she confirmed, and, forcing herself through a sad moment, added, 'We feature each other, but Belvia is blonde and beautiful.'

Dacre looked at her in some surprise. 'You surely don't imagine that you are not beautiful also?' he exclaimed, and she stared at him, surprised in turn. Did Marc's cousin think her beautiful?

She decided that she didn't want this conversation. 'Belvia was married at the beginning of October and—'

'She no longer lives at home?'

Josy shook her head. 'Not now. And I'm so happy for her. She didn't hesitate to come out when I needed her, when Marc—w-was killed.'

'His parents told me of the deep shock you were in.'

She didn't want to talk about that either—and then a sudden thought struck her. 'Will Monseir and Madame Paumier be visiting you here?'

'It is most unlikely,' he replied. 'Would it worry you if they did?'

She thought about it for a few moments. 'Only in so much as to see me might, perhaps, bring back memories of their son.'

'They have happy memories of him, Josy,' Dacre told her quietly. 'They have the happiest memory of all— that you made his life complete by marrying h—'

'*Don't*!' She couldn't take it. Oh, heavens, she was going to cry!

'Oh, *ma chère*. Forgive me.' Dacre's hand whipped across the table and he grasped hers firmly. Oddly, though, as he gripped her his strength seemed to pass from him to her, so that somehow Josy found that she had managed to conquer her fear of breaking down.

'It's all right. I'm sorry. I...' She pulled her hand away from his.

'It is nearly a year; I thought it might help you to talk about it,' her French host murmured compassionately.

She could never talk about it. Not that! Though perhaps Dacre, who had loved Marc too, might have a need not to shut him away as if he never had existed? 'Sometimes it's all right—other times...' She let it go, but was not totally surprised when he changed the subject.

'It is very remiss of me, but I've only just realised that we never got round to discussing your salary. I will—'

'Oh, I don't want paying!' Josy exclaimed. 'Grief, it's only a couple of horses—it's hardly work.'

He stared at her in amazement. 'But of course I must pay you!' he stated authoritatively.

Josy, for all that she was extremely shy, had a spark of spirit which on a few, albeit widely-spaced occasions in the past had ignited without any assistance or fore-knowledge from her at the most unexpected moments.

She pushed her chair back and was on her feet. 'I, *monsieur*,' she reminded him loftily, with something in her—she knew not what—objecting strongly to Dacre Banchereau talking so authoritatively to her, 'am family!' And with that, while Dacre, staring at her as if he couldn't believe it, got to his feet too, she left the room.

Josy went straight up to her room, and only when she was in that safe harbour did she sink down on the bed and, as if she couldn't believe it either, wondered, Had that been her? Had that been her timid little self?

She went to bed. My word, was there something magical about this place or was there something magical?

She had not expected to sleep well, but to her surprise she did. Even so, she was up at first light and was ashamed of her non-positive wish to be back home of yesterday. Positive—that was the way from now on. Dacre would be gone by tomorrow. In all likelihood he would leave for Paris today—and then she could settle down and enjoy being here.

On that thought she went and showered and, still thinking positive, donned jodhpurs and a fresh shirt and sweater. In the light of that lovely spring morning, she could hardly credit that last night she had haughtily bounced back at Dacre that she was family, thereby neither expecting nor wanting to be paid.

She left her room quietly and tripped lightly down the stairs and out through the front door. She breathed in the new spring day—it was good. Her boots crunched over the gravel as she went along the wide frontage of the building and, as quietly as she could, down the side of the large house.

There were a few outbuildings at the rear of the property, she observed—in fact a good many out-buildings—but no stables. Now where—?

'Going riding?'

She spun round. 'Oh, hello,' she gasped. Why, when she had been very conscious of the noise she had been making as she'd walked over the gravel, hadn't she heard him? She looked beyond Dacre and realised that he had come out a back way. 'I can't find the stables,' she owned up, glad to hear from the teasing sound of him that he wasn't holding her abrupt departure from the dinner-table last night against her.

'That's because they're a quarter of a mile away.' He smiled—it was almost a grin. Strangely her breath caught.

'Ah,' she said. 'Is my car garaged here?' she asked, pointing to a block of single-storeyed buildings.

'You wish to drive to the stables?'

'Oh, no. If you'll give me directions I'll walk. I just thought, with you saying you'd garaged my car, that it might be here.'

'Come, I'll show you.' And, so saying, Dacre took her over to the buildings and opened one of them up.

'Thank you,' she said on seeing her vehicle, glad to know where it was—not that she envisaged using it very much. 'If you could tell me where—'

'I'll come with you.'

'But it's early, and you haven't had breakfast.'

'Neither have you,' he replied and, teasingly, she felt sure—although she couldn't be entirely certain—he went on, 'What sort of "family" would I be if I allowed you to go on your own—on this, your first morning?'

'Should I apologise for my rudeness last night?' she wondered out loud.

'I shouldn't think so,' he replied, making her realise that she must have spoken her thoughts, and, leading her away from the outbuildings and along a newly grav-elled wide path, he said, 'Should I, perhaps, have written to your father?' This time he seemed to be wondering *his* thoughts out loud.

'No!' she exclaimed unequivocally. The one letter she herself had received from Dacre had been addressed to Mrs M Paumier. Thankfully her father hadn't been around when it had arrived. Though if he had he would have written 'not known' on it and either forgotten it or posted it back.

'You sound alarmed.' Dacre made no pretence of not noticing.

'My father wouldn't... Er—what would you want to write to him for?' She changed tack.

'A courtesy, no more, on the occasion of your ex-changing his roof for mine. Perhaps a note to assure him that I'll take every care of my cousin's widow would still not come amiss.'

'*No*!' she exclaimed again, more vehemently this time—and at her tone he halted. Josy stopped too, but as she looked at him so she saw from a quietly determined kind of look in his eyes that that heated no was not good enough. He wanted more.

'You're afraid of something?' he enquired, calm where she was far from calm.

'No, I'm not,' she denied; she didn't have to tell him if she didn't want to.

'What, then?'

Damn him! Dacre had stirred her to anger once before. She who seldom knew anger felt angry again. 'I've told you I'm twenty-three—hardly at the age when you need to write home to my parent to tell him I'm fine.'

'You don't think he'll be anxious about you?' Josy thought nothing of the kind. So long as Mrs Vale's cooking, cleaning and laundry service went on uninterrupted she doubted whether her father would give her more than a passing thought. 'Have you phoned to tell him of your safe arrival?' he pressed when she did not answer.

'I'll write,' she answered shortly.

And she felt she hated Dacre Banchereau when, looking her straight in the eye, he replied, 'Out of courtesy so will I.'

'No—you mustn't!' she flared.

'So tell me why.'

Damn him—damn him to hell. 'Because—because...' And damn him some more. 'Because—save for him knowing I've come to France to work with horses—my father won't have a clue who you are!' she said heatedly, two bright spots of angry pink colouring her normally pale skin.

'You haven't told him you were coming to your husband's family? That the man you—?'

'No, I haven't.'

'Why?'

She wriggled; she writhed; she hated Dacre with a vengeance. 'Because...' she ground out, recognising a tenacity in him that assured her he was not going to let the subject drop. 'B-because my father doesn't know I've got another family,' she railed, 'that I've had a husband—that I've been marr...' Her voice petered out—she wanted her words back. Dacre's astonishment was all too obvious.

'Your father doesn't know you've been married?' he queried incredulously.

'And I don't want you to tell him either!' she erupted—and was made to endure his scrutiny as he rocked back on his heels and studied her for long, silent moments.

'Oh, sweet Josy,' he drawled at length, 'who would have suspected that there was such depth in you, such anger in you, such—' he broke off, and, looking at her sparking brown eyes, chose his next words carefully 'such deceit?' he ended.

It was that word 'deceit' that got to her—as she later realised it had been meant to. But then all she knew as her spurt of anger refused to die was that she could not stand still under that charge. 'I didn't not tell him for me—but for Marc!' she retorted.

'My cousin asked you not to tell your father?' he questioned. 'I know Marc was reticent with people, but surely—?'

'It wasn't Marc's decision.'

'Yours?'

Josy, quietly seething, looked at him. But, short of her packing up and going home right this minute, she could see that there was nothing to do but tell him. Having got here, having spent a night under Dacre Banchereau's roof, she discovered that she felt reluctant to leave. 'You won't like it,' she told him tautly.

'I'll be the judge of that.'

Was he needling her on purpose? 'Very well,' she began sniffily, 'since you must know—my father would not have looked kindly on my marrying a mere groom.'

'Your father is a snob?'

In spades. She nodded. At one time she might have tried to cover for her parent, but after his last devious trick she felt she owed him little loyalty. 'I'm afraid so,' she agreed, and as all anger drained from her added, 'That was obvious when I suggested bringing Marc home to introduce him.' She paused as she remembered, but after taking a shaky breath she went on, 'Marc and my father never met. We got married with just my sister there to represent our families.'

Dacre wasn't goading her any more either as he inserted quietly, 'You had a flat to return to over the stables, I believe?' revealing that he knew some of their conversation with Marc's parents that evening of their wedding day.

'Yes. Belvia went and saw to everything when we got back, and kept my wedding a secret when I told her that I didn't want my insensitive father to know.'

'Is that the real reason why you do not wear a wedding ring?' he wanted to know.

It was only a part of it—a very small part of it—but she wasn't going to tell him that. She could not tell him or anyone else her feelings—that realisation that because she had never been a wife she had no right to wear it. 'It's as I told you,' she said, and went to walk on, and then found, when he placed a light, restraining hand on her arm, that he hadn't finished yet.

And that caused a flicker of annoyance to touch her, before he followed up with a cool, 'Didn't you know that Marc could have bought the stables where he worked if he'd so wished?'

'I didn't marry him for his money, if that's what you mean,' she retorted, and straight away something sharp and, thankfully, in French hit her ears as Dacre let fly with an exclamation indicating that clearly she had misunderstood him.

'Don't I already know that?' he bit out, reverting back to English. 'Don't his family know that, when you have refused all offers of financial assistance?'

'I have my own money,' she retorted stubbornly. She had replied politely not only to Monsieur and Madame Paumier's wish to see her provided for financially, but also to Marc's lawyers, who had written to say that she was a beneficiary of his estate. 'It's not a fortune by your standards, but my mother left me enough to be independent.'

Dacre looked at her long and hard, and then he charged toughly, 'Do you think you are being quite fair to Marc?' and Josy jetted into orbit.

'How *dare* you?' she raged, and, flinging his hand from her arm, regardless that she might be going in the wrong direction, she stormed away from him.

How dared he? she fumed. He knew absolutely nothing about it! She was going home. Dammit, no she wasn't. She would stick it out here if it killed her. This was her new life. She wasn't going running just because Marc's cousin was showing himself to be a brute of a man.

He'd be leaving today anyway—at the latest, tomorrow. She'd keep well out of his way meantime, and—with luck—perhaps he wouldn't show up again for another month.

Josy gradually came down out of orbit, to be faintly astounded that she had come so far out of her shell since she had arrived in France that she could feel and show the outrage of fury she had just experienced. Only then— aware that Dacre, no doubt silently thinking his own thoughts, was walking right beside her—was she able to accept that guilt over her part in her unconsummated marriage had made her rage, How *dare* you? at him. She had not been able to accept Marc as a husband, so how on earth could she accept anything that he as a husband had left her?

She was still feeling not too well disposed to the man walking with her when he enquired silkily, 'Have you always been shy?' And the oddest thing started to happen in her. Remembering her rage, her fury with him, her anything but shy How *dare* you?, even while she was still annoyed with him Josy felt she wanted to laugh.

She wouldn't, of course, though it was a fact that her lips twitched a little. She gave a small cough, just to show that he had no power at all to winkle out her sense of humour.

'One of these days I'm going to grow out of it,' she threatened solemnly, but could not resist a flick of a glance at him. To her amazement she saw that *his* lips were twitching.

A minute or so later a newly fenced paddock came into view, and after a short while they were at the stables and he was introducing her to two very well-behaved horses.

With a pang Josy thought of Hetty. But Hetty was being well looked after, and she was only here for six months. By that time—and already, if her spat with Dacre was anything to go by, the signs were good—she would be ready to take on the challenge of finding a job in England where she and Hetty could be together.

A feeling of near-contentment washed over her as she stroked and patted first Nina and then César. 'We'll saddle up, and I'll show you round this area,' Dacre decided after some minutes.

'I can go by myself,' Josy replied, thinking to exercise Nina first and then come back for César.

'You going shy on me again?' he teased.

'Where's the tack-room?'

They were out for about two hours. They spoke little as they walked and sometimes cantered their mounts, but up in the saddle Josy began to feel more and more at home, and as they cantered over fields and walked through woods—sometimes catching a glimpse of Dacre's stately house, sometimes not—so she realised it was common sense for him to ride with her this first time. Tomorrow she would be able to follow the same route, and soon, when she had found her bearings, she could start to explore other routes.

Her face was aglow with pleasure by the time they returned to the stables. But before she could dismount she saw that he had already dismounted and was coming over to her, looking up into her face. He looked pleased, she thought, but didn't know how *she* felt when he put up his arms as if to help her down.

She wanted to tell him that she did not need his help. But with her equilibrium fully restored after that lovely ride she hesitated. Somehow, especially after the way she had lost her temper with him—and she could still barely credit that that had been her—it seemed churlish and as if she were sulking over the comments he had made.

She cocked a leg over the saddle and leaned down to catch a hold of his arms—and just at that moment Nina did a sideways shuffle and Josy went pitching forward.

But Dacre caught her. He went a shade off balance but, his arms coming round her, he caught her and held her fast while he regained his balance. Josy had to lean her body hard against his so that she too could get her balance, and just as Dacre glanced down into her face she went scarlet.

He stilled, held her motionless as he stared, fascinated, as the colour rioted in her face. Her breath caught, her heart thundered, and as wild panic hit she felt that she was going to faint. She looked up into a pair of grey eyes that were watching her—and pushed him away.

Dacre took a couple of casual steps from her, and while she was a tangle of agitation, striving for calm, remarked, 'I've got a busy schedule; we'd better see about unsaddling.'

'I'll do it,' she promptly volunteered, and was amazed that when she was feeling so emotionally all over the place inside her voice should come out sounding so natural.

'They'll need feeding too, and turning out into the paddock.'

'I can do that too. It's what I'm here for.'

He consulted his watch. 'Would you mind?' he glanced up to enquire.

'Not a bit,' she replied, and was a lot relieved when, staying only to unsaddle his mount, he then went striding back along the path to the house.

Josy watched him go, and discovered that she was trembling a little. Oh, heavens, how she wished that he

had left her to get down from Nina by herself. To help
her off was a courteous thing to have done, of course,
but oh, how she wished he hadn't bothered. She could
still feel his body pressed against hers. It disturbed her—
he disturbed her—and she didn't want to be disturbed.

CHAPTER THREE

DACRE had left for Paris by the time Josy returned to the house, and she was glad about that. Somehow he had a knack of causing ripples, not to say—and she recalled how furious he had made her—the occasional tidal wave in the still waters of her life.

Indeed, so unsettled had he made her—she didn't want any man's arms around her, even if she was fully aware that he had *had* to catch hold of her—she had taken her time in feeding, checking the automatic water supply, and grooming Nina and César before turning them loose in the paddock.

Not that there had turned out to be any need to rush back to the house, because, as if he'd known that she would not be in any hurry to go back but would return rather than offend Agathe, who might be preparing a midday meal, Dacre had sent a picnic. Agathe's husband Franck had pedalled up with it on the back of his bicycle while she'd been checking the water trough in the paddock.

He'd introduced himself and handed her the basket, and waited while she lifted the cover. 'Oh!' she'd exclaimed in surprise, the sight of a vacuum flask causing her to realise that the lunch had arrived. '*Merci, monsieur*,' she'd thanked him shyly.

She had been positively beamed at before he'd wished her, '*Bon appétit, madame*,' and cycled off.

There was an air of recent modernisation about the stable block she'd rather thought when, suddenly aware that she was hungry, she'd gone to the washroom to scrub her hands and had noticed the pristine condition of the porcelain and piping.

Once outside again she'd taken her picnic basket over to where a newish-looking, long wooden bench with a back to it had been most conveniently placed. And, seated with the paddock in front of her and lovely countryside about, she'd begun to grow calmer again. It was truly beautiful here.

Much later she'd investigated what else the well-equipped tack-room housed, besides saddles and bridles, and had spent an energetic hour or two polishing already shiny leather.

When at half-past six she returned to the house she recalled how Dacre had remarked on his busy schedule. She thought that she could take it that he had only left Paris in order to be at the estate when she'd arrived, as he had promised he would be and had matters in Paris that required his attention even on a Sunday.

As she expected, Dacre had left, and, feeling more relaxed knowing that, Josy went up to her room, feeling pleasantly tired and with nothing more strenuous in mind than a soak in the bath,

However, she had no sooner entered her room than she saw with a start that her car keys were on her dressing-table, and beside them a note. Dacre had been to her room.

Agathe will serve you dinner at eight every evening unless you wish to alter that. If you have any problem, no matter how small, please contact me. Treat my home as your home.

In case she had forgotten to bring his Paris number

with her, Dacre had jotted down both his office number
and his Paris number. He had signed it 'D'.

That was when Josy decided that she definitely liked
her cousin-in-law. While he might wreck her equilibrium, and draw from her a person she hardly recognised, and while she might prefer it not to be that way,
and, therefore, appreciate his absence, it had been kind
and generous of him to tell her to treat his home as her
home. Josy, in an easier frame of mind, went and had
her bath.

There followed a week in which she made the ac-
quaintance of two ladies from the village who came to
clean—Edith and Lilas—and also a fiftyish man by the
name of Georges, who gardened.

Between Franck and Georges, Josy had not the
smallest worry with the horses. For either they loved
horses too, or had had instructions from their employer,
because one or other of them was always there to help
her with Nina and César when she returned from exercising them. As, too, if she was overlong at the stables,
would one or other of them come cycling casually by.

She wanted to tell them that she was all right, that
they had no need to check on her, that she could very
well unsaddle the horses on her own. But she did not
feel that she could countermand any orders Dacre had
given, and, in any case, she knew full well that her French
was just not up to any involved conversation.

On Tuesday her twin rang. Josy was in the dining-
room enjoying her evening meal when Agathe came in,
and out of all that she said Josy picked up, '... telé-
phone, madame.'

Why her heart should suddenly beat faster at the
thought that Dacre was waiting for her to come to the
phone Josy had no idea, but she left the dining-room

and went out into the hall, where the nearest phone was lying off its rest on an antique table.

'Hello?' she said, feeling a mite shaky. And at once felt her equilibrium return on hearing her sister's voice.

'Are you all right?' Belvia enquired anxiously. 'You sound nervous.'

'I'm absolutely fine!' Josy replied, a smile in her voice. Aware that her sister would worry about her if she couldn't convince her, she added, 'I didn't know who was calling, but I'll admit I wasn't looking forward to trying to converse with someone in French.'

'I know what you mean. I don't know who answered the phone, but it was only when a string of French hit my ears that I realised I might have a few problems. I cheated, I'm afraid. I just said, *Parlez-vous anglais, madame*? I think I was told to hold on a moment, which I did, and here you are—so top marks to whoever it was.'

'It was Agathe, Dacre's housekeeper.'

'How is he—Dacre?'

'Oh, he went back to Paris on Sunday.'

'And you got there without any problems? I wanted to ring you on Saturday. Sunday and Monday too, come to think of it—' Belvia laughed '—but decided to let you settle in first. Coping?'

'Very well,' Josy replied. 'It's lovely here.'

She *was* coping very well, too, she realised, by the time Thursday rolled around. Not that looking after just two horses could be called work—as she had told Dacre.

She had started to feel relaxed too—unbelievably relaxed, given the few short days she had been here. Was it just the calm, the tranquillity of this lovely place in part of the valley of the Loire? Or did the fact that she had broken away from her father and his dominance play some part?

Whatever it was, when Friday turned out to be a dull, rainy day she went down to the stables to talk to Nina and César and to feed them and decided against exercising them. That afternoon she decided to take her car out of its garage. She drove in to Saumur, with its majestic fourteenth-century château built on a promontory and overlooking the lovely town below.

Yet, as lovely as the town was, Josy no sooner got there than she had a feeling of wanting to be back again at Dacre's home. She stayed long enough to purchase a picture postcard, however, and, taking an afternoon cup of tea, she addressed it to her father to advise him of her safe arrival. It only struck her how independent of him she had become when she suddenly found that she was thinking that perhaps she would consider writing a letter to him at some later date.

On her return Josy met Agathe, and they smiled and greeted each other and, as Hetty had been in her thoughts a lot that day, Josy went to the telephone and rang the stables.

'Tracey?' she enquired when the phone was answered.

'The same.'

'It's Josy Fereday. I'm in France. I wondered if Hetty was all right?'

'Never better,' Tracey assured her. 'Spoilt to death, of course, and missing her mum, but otherwise great.'

Josy felt a knife turn at 'missing her mum', but these six months would soon pass, and if Hetty really was missing her she could pop back to England for a few days to see her every now and then.

'You've got my number here if you need it?' she checked, and spoke to Tracey for another minute or so, then came away from the phone realising that, should she nip back to England for a few days to see Hetty, she had a decided aversion to returning to the home that she had shared with her father.

She was in her room getting ready to go down to dinner that night, with the same subject still on her mind, when it dawned on her that now that the break was made it was total. There was no going back. She knew then that whatever happened—even should she not be able to find a live-in job—she would never return to live in her old home. Suddenly she was starting to be the positive person she wanted to be. And she liked it. Then the phone in her room rang.

Startled, she stared at it. It had never rung before. Was Belvia phoning again? Had Agathe switched the call through? Josy went over to the phone and picked it up. 'Hello?' she said—and was all at once not positive about anything any more.

'You've had a good week, Josy?' Dacre enquired.

She felt breathless. 'Oh—yes,' she answered.

'With nothing to worry you?'

'No. Nothing.' She wished she could think of something to say—something positive—but could think of nothing.

'The horses are well?'

'Oh, yes. Yes, they are.'

'Then I will not keep you.'

Her brain sprang into action. 'Are you coming home tomorrow?' she asked in a rush.

There was a pause, a silence. Then he asked, 'You wish me to?' And Josy felt exceedingly embarrassed, and as if she had asked him to come.

'No,' she denied sharply. And, not knowing why the dickens she had asked—for it was no concern of hers what he did—she endured more agonised seconds of embarrassment, with no way to retrieve that sharp, No, while Dacre obviously considered if he wanted to make the trip from Paris or not.

Not, it seemed. Though she doubted whether her wanting him there or not made a scrap of difference when he at last replied, 'Then if you have no problems I will stay in Paris. *Au revoir*, Josy.'

'Bye,' she answered, and put down the phone feeling gauche and awkward, but overall generally glad that she would not see him that weekend.

Some of her new-found confidence had returned by Monday of the following week. On Thursday she again drove into Saumur, and on Friday she drove up to the Ecole Nationale d'Equitation, and watched in awe as the Cadre Noir put their splendid horses through their paces.

She was still reliving all she had seen in her room that evening. But as she started to get bathed and changed for dinner all thoughts of horses and anything else had gone from her mind.

She glanced nervously at the phone. Dacre had rung around this time last Friday. Would he ring again to-night? What would she say if he again asked if she wanted him to come home? In truth she had no idea. Somehow the positive side she thought she had found had started to waver again, and she didn't know if she wanted to see him or not.

Dacre had not rung by the time she was ready to leave her room. Nor did he ring while she was at dinner. Josy returned to her room knowing that he was not going to ring now. And why would he? It was his house; he could come and go as he pleased. And, in any case, she thought, recalling that last Friday he had as good as said that if the horses were well he would not keep her, he had only rung last Friday to check that Nina and César were all right.

When later she climbed into bed Josy had recalled a lot of other things too—among them how furious he had made her. She could only remember being so outraged once before—she had been fifteen, and had just witnessed her father striking her mother.

Josy slept very badly that night. She got out of bed early on Saturday morning, glad to leave it. The night seemed to have gone on for ever. She went to take a shower and, as if trying to outstrip unwanted thoughts that continued to pursue her, she hurried to the breakfast-room, had a swift breakfast of croissant, apricot jam and coffee, and went quickly the quarter of a mile to the stables.

As ever, both Nina and César were uncomplicated and glad to see her, as she was to see them. But for once, as she stroked and patted them and gave them an apple each to start the day, she could not lose herself totally in their company. Uppermost in her mind were still haunted thoughts of her abhorrence of physical violence—and her fear of it.

Sometimes she took the horses out together, riding one out and the other back, but that morning she felt filled with a restless kind of energy. To take them both would slow her down. She did a few chores and then, intending to take César out later, she saddled up Nina.

Josy was about two miles away from home and concentrating on anything but her riding when Nina stumbled in a pothole—and Josy fell off. Staring disbelievingly at Nina from her sitting position on the ground, Josy laughed ruefully. But she was yet more dis-

believing when the well-behaved and lovable Nina, either
thinking to have a game or perhaps thinking that she
would be fed almost as soon as she returned home, took
off.

'Well!' Josy exclaimed, watching helplessly as the
horse cantered back the way she had come.

She was about to get up and start the two-mile walk
back when she heard the sound of a light aircraft
overhead. She watched it for some seconds, leaning back
on her elbows. Then she lost interest. But, instead of
getting to her feet as she had intended, she lay there, as
if hoping that some of the serenity of her surroundings
would rub off on to her. Either Georges or Franck would
be there to look after Nina when she got home, she could
guarantee.

Josy lay down, the sun warm on her face. She closed
her eyes, but only for a few minutes as she tried to think
of nothing and found that impossible. Thoughts of Marc
penetrated. Dear Marc—she should never have married
him. Guilt swamped her. Guilt she didn't need. Guilt she
couldn't cope with. Think of something else.

An image of her father came to her, his face contorted
with fury. She wiped him from her mind, and thought
of Dacre Banchereau. But somehow she didn't want to
think about him, either. He disturbed her, she acknowledged, and made herself think of Belvia instead. She
thought of her sister's goodness, her caring, and began
to relax.

'*Josy! Josy!*' She felt comfortable and didn't want to
wake up.

But wake up she did—in a startled and terrified way.
She had not been dreaming! Someone *had* been shouting
her name! Barely realising that she had been asleep, Josy
came to rapidly, to hear a volley of French in her ears,

while at the same time she opened her eyes at the touch
of an exploring hand in the neck of her shirt.

In an instant, even as she recognised that Dacre was
somehow home, she was pushing him frantically away
while at the same time yelling, 'Get away from me!'

'I was feeling for a pulse!'

'Don't touch me!' she shrieked, on her feet and moving
backwards, her eyes fixed on his face. Vaguely she
realised that he seemed paler than she remembered.

'I thought you were dead!'

'Well, I'm not!' she threw at him, her panic starting
to subside; she had been mistaken—his colour now
looked normal.

'I can see that you're not,' he retorted, and, with some
utterance in French, added, 'My God—there's passion
in you, Josy Paumier!'

Abruptly she turned her back on him. Passion she
knew there was not. And, while she might have a legal
right to be called Paumier, she knew that she was not
morally entitled to that name either. And she was hating
Dacre Banchereau that he could—even unknowingly—
refer so easily to matters which were such an unhappy
source of unrest within her.

She wanted him to go, to leave her in peace, but
guessed that she should have known better.

'Come, here is César.'

She turned, noticed César for the first time, and
realised that Dacre must have called him from wherever
he'd left him. 'What do you mean—"here is César"?'
she asked, belligerent in her trauma.

Dacre eyed her steadily, either assessing or not liking
her tone—she couldn't decide which. 'Get on him,' he
clipped—not liking, she realised.

'No!' she retorted. Nothing on God's earth was going to have her riding in tandem with him.

'I wasn't thinking of riding the horse with you, if that's what you're afraid of!' he snarled, clearly having read her mind.

And she didn't like that. But, more, she positively hated that word 'afraid'. And she hated him that he could suggest that she might be afraid of any physical contact with another human being—hated him so much that she wasn't thinking but only feeling when, furious with him for a second time, she charged past him like a flash, was up in the saddle and away.

Damn him; damn him to hell, she fumed as she set César to the gallop. Let *him* walk the two miles back. She hoped it came on to rain. A cloudburst would suit her nicely. A lightning bolt wouldn't come amiss either.

It did not come on to rain but remained a blissful spring-turning-to-summer day. Nor did Josy gallop César for long. Indeed, by the time the stables came into view she had slowed him to a walk and, her temper spent, she was quite bewildered to know what had come over her.

Franck was at the stables; he seemed relieved to see her, and she felt more guilt to think that although she had not meant to fall asleep, she had done so, causing him alarm when a riderless Nina had come home.

'I'm sorry, Franck,' she apologised, and guessed that he understood from her solemn expression that she was not too happy with herself just then. He smiled anyhow, and she thought that meant he had forgiven her when he helped her unsaddle César and look after him.

By the time both horses were attended to and were out in the paddock Josy had surfaced from the mind-numbing confusion of her behaviour to be dreadfully contrite, for, as she ceased trying to fathom the unfathomable about this new and fiery person her cousin-in-law seemed to cause to explode in her, so she began to think of matters from his side of things.

By the time Dacre appeared and neared where she was standing Josy was feeling very much ashamed of herself. Oh, heavens, leave alone the fact that the cousin he'd loved had been killed in a riding accident, Dacre must have wondered if history had been repeating itself when Franck had told him that Nina had come home without her.

He must have saddled up César straight away and come looking for her. Lord knew what his thoughts had been when, from high up on the back of César, he had spotted her lying there, still, not moving. Of course his first action before he did anything else on getting to her had been to check for a pulse in her neck, to see if she was still alive. And what had she done but shrieked at him like some demented fishwife?

Dacre was about ten yards away when, mortified, she moved in his direction. Inexplicably, considering the very vocal shrew she had been, she felt shy again. But, shy or not, it had to be done.

She approached him and stopped. He saw her, looked down at her from his aloof height and, without saying a word, carried on walking.

Josy stared after him; she wanted to call his name, to halt him, but that tedious shyness held her tongue captive. And that was when her new world started to shatter about her. His aloofness, his going by without a word said it all. Dacre wanted her to leave!

Her breath caught on that dreadful thought and she knew, for all that she had been there for only two weeks, that she did not want to leave. Her heart sank. She did not question the fact; she just knew that it was so. Just as she knew that she was too proud to stay anywhere where she was not wanted.

She went and checked the paddock. Nina and César were passing that part of the day in the plentiful supply of shade amongst some trees over at the far side. She went and washed her hands, after which, in a perturbed frame of mind, she started to walk back to the house.

Dacre was nowhere to be seen when she went indoors, but she hung around in the drawing-room for ten minutes just in case he came in. When he did not she decided to go up to her room to shower and change—perhaps she'd feel a shade more confident if she smelt less horsey.

She had just reached the landing at the top of the stairs, however, when a door a couple of rooms up from her own opened, and Dacre came from a bedroom which she assumed to be his. From the damp look to his dark hair she guessed that he had already showered and changed.

He saw her at once, and halted. And as warm colour seared her cheeks she knew she had to go on. She had no more idea of what she was going to say then than she had when she'd decided she must go and see him, but pride refused to let her stay where she was not wanted and forced her to go forward.

She drew level with him, saw that he was watching her with steady grey eyes, and blurted out, 'I expect you want me to go?'

He looked a degree startled, though his tone was calm as he replied, 'Go? Where?'

Was he playing with her? Involuntarily her chin tilted a proud fraction. 'I thought you might want me to leave.' She forced the words out.

Again she had to suffer his steady look. Then he asked softly, 'Why would I want you to leave?'

She stared at him, all large brown eyes. 'I thought—
me leaving you to walk home and everything...' she
managed lamely, joy starting to enter her being at the
realisation that, by the sound of it, she had got it all
wrong and Dacre hadn't taken exception to her
behaviour.

'You are my family, Josy, are you not?' he answered,
and to her delight smiled a smile full of charm as he
teased, 'Do you not know that in families one is privi-
leged to leave other family members to walk a solitary
two miles home?'

'Oh, Dacre,' she murmured involuntarily. And, even
though her mouth curved upwards in a smile which
denied the apology, she said, 'I'm sorry.'

She saw his glance flick from her eyes to her smiling
mouth, and observed the way he seemed fascinated by
it—that was when she realised how seldom she smiled.
No wonder he was fascinated. It was high time she
lightened up. 'Well, don't do it again,' he ordered with
a mock severity that made her want to laugh. He turned
away, seemed about to go on his way, then turned back
to enquire, as if it were his responsibility, 'Did you get
down from Nina voluntarily or did she unseat you?'

'My fault alone,' Josy quickly assured him. 'I wasn't
paying any attention to her or what I was doing when
she stumbled and we lightly parted company.'

'You're not hurt?'

'Not even my pride,' she laughed, and it was true, and
Dacre flicked one more glance to her mouth then turned
abruptly about.

'Take a hot bath just the same,' he ordered over
his shoulder.

Josy turned away and went to her room. She didn't
want a hot bath, she thought rebelliously, and was under

the shower when she paused stock-still to wonder what was happening to her. This wasn't her, not the Josy Fereday she knew, laughing, mutinous—her breath caught—alive!

She almost gasped at that last thought, but could not or would not work it out. She reached for her shampoo and drowned further thoughts by concentrating on washing her long strawberry-tinted fair hair.

She decided when lunchtime came around that she did not want to join Dacre for the midday meal. It was only the thought that she was likely to draw more attention to herself if she didn't appear at the lunch table that made her go.

And then she discovered that she need not have worried anyhow because Dacre was not there. By signs and bits of French Josy thought she had conveyed to Agathe that she would wait for *monsieur* before she began her meal, only to translate Agathe's admittedly slowed-down French to comprehend that Dacre would not be in to lunch, that *monsieur* was out seeing friends.

Whether Agathe had said *amis* for male friends or *amies* for female friends, Josy was sure she was not so interested that she wanted to find out. She was not very hungry, she discovered, but she ate what she could, since Agathe had troubled to cook for her, and afterwards she returned to her room to change. She felt restless again and, if Franck hadn't beaten her to it, she would go and muck out the stables.

Josy returned to the house at six-thirty and went straight to have the hot bath which Dacre had ordered earlier that day. She spent some time considering her wardrobe after her bath and opted for a plain, lavender-coloured dress that looked nothing on its hanger yet looked good on.

At five to eight she left her room, wondering if Dacre would be in to dinner or out again with his friends or, more likely, some lady-friend. No doubt he had lady-friends here as well as in Paris. Not that it was any business of hers. Not that she cared.

But, most oddly, Josy discovered that while at lunchtime she had not wanted his company she now would not have minded someone to chat with over a meal. Chat with? Grief, she had always preferred her own company!

She remembered thinking before that there was something magical—a magical air—about the place. It certainly had a lot to answer for. Any further thoughts on the matter, however, swiftly departed when it suddenly occurred to her that there might be more than Dacre for company. What if his *amie* was dining with them?

At one time that thought alone might have seen her hastening back to her room but—and again she hardly knew herself—while, admittedly, she had to pause at the drawing-room door to gather her courage together before she could open it, open it she did.

'Ah, Josy!' Dacre greeted her. And he was alone.

'I'm not late?' She knew she wasn't, but needed to say something.

'Not unless you insist on having a drink first,' he teased.

Oh, she did like him. 'No, thanks,' she replied, and silently owned to feeling a little breathless when, taking a light hold of her elbow, he escorted her to the dining-room.

Josy was tucking into a starter of mussels in parsley butter before she said another word. And then it was only in response to Dacre's, 'No sign of a bruise, I hope?'

For a second she wasn't with him. Then she remembered that she had come off Nina that morning. 'Not one,' she answered.

'You went back to the stables this afternoon?' he enquired conversationally.

'It's lovely there. Did you have that bench put there? It looks quite new.'

'You may blame me,' he invited with charm, and, oddly, her heart gave a little flutter.

'It's in exactly the right spot,' she murmured, and as a thought suddenly struck her she grasshoppered on to something else and said, 'I saw—this morning when I was—um—taking my ease—I saw a small aircraft go over. It wasn't you, was it?'

'There's an airfield quite close, and very convenient,' he replied, giving her a warm look, and she promptly ran out of questions. But not so he. 'You feel—um—settled in with us now?' he enquired.

Given that there seemed to be an uneasy restlessness growing in her, and given that in two short weeks she was losing sight of the Josy she had always been, she rather thought she had settled in amazingly well.

'Yes, thank you,' she replied politely, and found a smile for Agathe when she came in to remove their used dishes and to deliver a most appetising chicken casserole that was worthy of a much more splendid name.

Dacre poured some wine, and as Agathe left the room, enquired, 'Have you been homesick at all?'

In all honesty she had to confess that she hadn't—confess to herself, that was. 'My twin left home when she married—as I told you. Seven months ago now. So I've got used to her not being around much. But Belvia phoned me here. And I rang the stables where my horse is. I miss her a little,' she added.

'Hetty.'

'You remember Hetty?'

'*Naturellement*!' He smiled, but, a still kind of look came to him. 'You mention your sister and your horse.' He paused, and then asked quietly, 'Do you not miss your father?'

'I...' She hesitated, and all at once became aware that, having lived in the same house with her father all her life, not only did she not miss her parent one tiny bit but she seldom thought about him. 'You make me feel guilty!' she exclaimed.

'Because you do not miss him?' She nodded. 'Forgive me—that was not my intention,' Dacre apologised at once, and, looking steadily at her for a few moments, he quietly asked, 'Was he a good father to you, Josy?'

Yes, she wanted to say. Oh, yes, wonderful. But Edwin Fereday had not been a good father, nor did he deserve loyalty, and when she opened her mouth to lie to Dacre she suddenly discovered that she could not lie to him.

'No,' she mumbled, and decided to leave it at that.

Only she had reckoned without Dacre who, on hearing her reply, did not seem to want to leave it there. 'He—beat you?' he enquired, still in that same quiet tone.

Josy stared down at her plate and shook her head to indicate that she did not want this conversation. Dacre said nothing, but nor did he carry on eating. For all his quiet way of speaking it seemed he was determined on more of an answer than that. A silence stretched, and Josy debated leaving the table and returning to her room.

Then incredibly she heard her own voice say, 'Just the once.'

Startled, she could hardly believe that she had answered. She made a small movement prior to getting up from the table, but, in doing so, glanced up and across to Dacre. He was sitting as silent as before. Silent—and waiting. But there was something in the grey depths of his eyes that was warm and encouraging—as if he knew that there was more to it than her having been lightly slapped for some childhood naughtiness.

And somehow Josy found that she had subsided back into her seat. 'Tell me about it,' he requested, his voice soft now, soothing. She stared at him. There was something slightly hypnotic about him. 'I am family, *petite*,' he reminded her gently.

Some family confidences were best kept to oneself, she decided. But as the seconds ticked by she replied, 'Th-there isn't a lot to tell.'

'How old were you?'

'Fifteen,' she answered, and, as the silence stretched, added, 'He was always aggressive, my father.' She stopped, yet somehow, as if a dam was starting to burst, she did not seem able to stop. 'For the most part he ignored us—me, Belvia and my mother.' Josy took a shaky intake of breath, and the dam fractured a little more. 'Then one Saturday Bel had gone swimming and I'd been to my music lesson. And when I went home there was an almighty row going on upstairs. I knew my parents were having a fierce verbal battle about something. I—' She broke off; she couldn't go on.

'But it wasn't purely verbal?' suggested a quiet, barely accented voice.

Again she shook her head. She didn't want to say any more. 'I—c-can't cope with physical aggression,' she whispered.

'But you did,' he gently prompted.

This time she nodded. And, as though speaking to herself, found that she was adding, 'I didn't want to hear them rowing. I went to the outer door. I thought I'd go and meet Belvia at the swimming pool. Then I heard a thud, a slap, the sound of my mother crying out. I don't remember anything after that but I suppose I must have rushed up the stairs, because the next thing I knew I was in my parents' bedroom.'

Words were pouring from her now—pent-up words she didn't seem able to stop, released words. 'My father was hitting my mother. I charged in between them and he began hitting me—he sent me flying across the room.' She gasped then, almost as if she could still feel the physical pain, the mental scars she still carried.

She felt her hands taken in a warm clasp and blinked, and saw that Dacre was sitting on a dining-chair next to her and was holding her hands. She had no idea when he had moved from his seat opposite or that she had turned towards him.

'You're nearly there,' he murmured softly.

'I—don't—want to say any more,' she choked.

'There's not much more, is there?' he sensitively invited.

'No, I suppose not,' she acknowledged slowly. 'I'm—er—all right now,' she told him, realising only then that she must have sounded quite distressed, and that Dacre, as sensitive as she had thought him, had left his seat to try to give what comfort he could.

She pulled her hands from his hold and he let her go, and, after a glance at her pale face, he went back to where he had been sitting—and Josy made every effort to control how shaky she was feeling.

'You charged in between your parents, you said,' he probed quietly when it seemed that he judged she was up to continuing. 'And he beat you.'

For the first time ever in the eight years that had elapsed since that dreadful afternoon she revealed, 'I hit him too.'

'You hit your father?'

'He was hitting my mother. I think I must have flipped because I went for him again, and the next thing I remember, my mother was pulling me from him and getting her and me some space from him. She had just received a private inheritance, and for the first time in her life was independent of him,' Josy explained. 'But I had never seen her so angry, nor so determined, when she told him that if he ever laid a finger on me again—or her, for that matter—then, regardless of the damage such publicity would cause him and his business, she would sue him for assault.'

'Your father—he never hit either of you again?'

'He is, I'm afraid, a bully. And like all bullies he backed off when he could see that, mainly because of me, my mother really meant what she said.'

'Your mother—she was the opposite of him,' Dacre stated.

'She was wonderful,' Josy agreed.

'She died when you were sixteen,' he commented.

'Marc's parents told you?'

Dacre nodded. 'You were a very brave young woman to try to protect your mother the way you did.'

'Oh, I don't know about that. Being brave is doing something that terrifies you, don't you think?' And, not waiting for an answer, she said, 'I wasn't terrified; I wasn't even thinking.'

'You just raced up the stairs and got in between them.' Dacre smiled. 'All of which,' he added, his smile gone as his grey eyes stayed on her, 'has left its mark on you.'

'Oh, I don't...' she began to deny.

'Your reserve—'

'I've always been shy,' she butted in, and suddenly became aware that at one time she had been so shy that she would never have butted in on what anyone was saying. 'Well, I was till I came here.' She smiled a little self-consciously.

'You still are.' He grinned as Agathe came in again. 'Mmm, a little cheese before your pudding?'

When Josy went to bed that night she feared that she might lie awake for hours reliving yet again the horrors of that time eight years ago. Yet, strangely, she went to sleep almost as soon as her head touched her pillow. Her last waking thought was, What was it about Dacre? She had never told a living soul what she had told him—what was it about the man?

CHAPTER FOUR

JOSY still found it incredible in the week that followed that she could have revealed to Dacre all she had about her father. It seemed to her not only incredible but unbelievable, when that secret had been locked up in her for so long, that she had opened up and told him all she had.

She was still puzzling out how it had all come about. Perhaps she had given away a hint that she and her father were not close in her admission that she did not miss him. It had brought forth Dacre's intuitive question of, 'Was he a good father to you?' anyhow.

But, whatever, while nothing seemed to take away the heavy burden of guilt she carried over Marc, Josy owned that she felt better about that dreadful scene eight years ago since she had shared it with Dacre.

He came home again at the weekend, but Nina had a slight cough and, having isolated her in the end stable of the block of four, putting César at the other end, Josy was more interested in staying near to the stables than in staying around the house.

She did make it for dinner on Saturday evening, though. 'This is the first time I've seen you today,' Dacre remarked when, on the stroke of eight, in a white shirt and a floral skirt—the first things to hand after her brief shower—she went quickly down the stairs.

'Er—hello,' she greeted him, and knew her rush not to keep anyone waiting was the reason for her breathlessness when Dacre, his hands coming to her arms, drew her to him and kissed first one cousinly cheek and then the other. 'Have you been to the stables?' she asked as they walked to the dining-room.

'Several times,' he replied drily.

'Oh, I'm sorry. Did you want to see me about anything in particular? Nina's got a bit of a cough, you see, and in between checking on her I've taken César for several long walks to keep him away from her.'

'I'll get someone in to help you,' Dacre decreed promptly.

'There's no need for that!' she declared, giving Agathe a warm smile when she came in with a soup tureen and went out again.

'Why isn't there? I'm not allowed to pay you, so why shouldn't I be allowed to pay someone to make your day easier?'

'Franck and Georges are always about if I need them,' she retaliated, amazed to realise that she was arguing with him—she who would run a mile from an argument! 'And, anyway, I like working on my own. Not that it's work,' she added hastily, and received a disgruntled look for her trouble.

Josy did not linger after her meal but returned to the stables. She discovered she had company, albeit silent company on the way back. She wanted to apologise to Dacre if she had done anything wrong but, in all honesty, couldn't think of anything she should say sorry for.

'I think Nina sounds a bit better.' She found her tongue as they went into the house. 'But if you wouldn't mind I'd like the vet to take a look at her.'

'I'll arrange it,' he clipped out, and Josy went to bed, relieved that the vet would call but feeling very mixed up about Dacre.

She had a restless night, and was up earlier than usual on Sunday morning and down at the stables checking on Nina. She was in the middle of crooning sweet nothings in the mare's ears when a droll voice suggested 'Why don't you bring your bed down here?'

A smile started deep inside her. She did not like to be bad friends, and it sounded as though—whatever her crime had been—Dacre had forgiven her.

She turned about, her eyes laughing. She hadn't been mistaken; Dacre's good humour had awakened with him—she could tell from the slight upturn at the corner of his rather splendid mouth. 'I didn't wake you up—leaving...?' Splendid mouth! Grief, where had that thought come from?

'I seem to require as little sleep as you,' he returned pleasantly. 'I was in my study, leaving a message on the horse doctor's answering machine, when you went by the window. How is she?'

'Definitely better. But I should still like the vet to see her.'

It was Dacre who exercised César that morning, leaving Josy with Nina. He had soon returned and gone back to the house and it was nearing noon when he drove down with a man a few years older than herself whom he introduced as the vet. And, while Josy started to feel quite awkward that Monsieur Gramache had been called out on a Sunday, when the next day would have done quite as well, the vet examined the mare.

'I will leave you some medicine; she will be well again in two or three days.' The vet, clearly preferring the look of Josy to Nina, turned to her to smile. His accent was strong but his English good.

'Thank you.' She smiled in turn, and, having felt at ease with him when discussing Nina, was ready to retreat when his smile lingered on her.

'I'll drive back to the house with you, *monsieur*,' Dacre said curtly, authoritatively. '*Madame* Paumier will want to settle the horse.'

'I will call again on Wednesday, *madame*.' The vet smiled again.

Josy looked from him to a not-very-pleased-looking Dacre, then Nina coughed and she forgot both of them.

Nina was better by Wednesday, but Josy was glad to see when the vet arrived that Franck was busy near by, giving the already pristine food store another coat of whitewash.

'Would you like me to check both horses while I'm here?' the vet asked.

It seemed a good idea. 'I'd be glad if you would, *monsieur*,' she replied.

'My first name is Regis,' he hinted, with a winning smile.

'Oh, yes,' she mumbled.

'And you are?'

'Mmm . . .' It seemed utterly ridiculous not to tell him. 'Josy,' she answered. 'And that,' she said, pointing to the horse who was having a little trot in the paddock, 'is César.'

Regis Gramache made his examinations, pronounced both horses fit and, telling Josy of his very early start that day as they walked back from the paddock, hinted at coffee. Oh, grief, she had an idea that the vet wanted to have a little flirt; she had small idea how to handle it.

She looked over to the food store, where Franck was taking a breather and, knowing that the small kitchenette off the washroom was now thoughtfully equipped

by Agathe with the makings for coffee and tea, called
'*Café*, Franck?'

She made coffee for them both, and left the two men
while she went and took Nina down to the paddock.

Her sister phoned her that evening just for a chat, and
it was lovely talking to her. But it endorsed for Josy
again that she had made the right decision in leaving
England for a while. She knew Belvia was concerned for
her and she didn't want that. Josy wanted nothing to
worry her sister ever again.

Saturday, for no reason that Josy could think of, seemed
to take a long time to come around. Only when she heard
the sound of a light aircraft overhead early that morning
did she realise that she had been listening for Dacre
without being fully aware of it.

It need not necessarily have been him, she knew, but
she felt almost light-hearted when, getting down from
Nina after taking her out for a canter, she saw that Dacre
had come down to the stables.

'*Bonjour*, Dacre,' she greeted him, and he came over.

'We'll have you speaking it like a native yet.' He
smiled, took a hold of her arms, and, looking deep into
her large brown eyes, murmured, '*Bonjour*, Josy,' and,
his head coming forward, he kissed her cheeks.

'I—er—thought I heard your plane,' she commented,
stepping back, feeling slightly flustered.

For a few silent moments he studied her. 'And I heard
that you make pretty good coffee,' he answered.

'Ah,' she said, and as Franck appeared from nowhere
and Dacre handed him Nina's reins so that he could look
after her added, 'You've been talking with Franck.'

'Going to make me some?'

'Of course,' she said, and led the way to the kitchenette.

'You're going to have coffee with me?' he asked as he took his ease on a wooden chair while Josy got busy making some coffee. 'Or,' he tacked on as an after-thought, 'are you going to leave me to drink mine with my odd-job man, like you did the vet?'

'Oh, heavens—was I very rude?' she asked.

His answer was to laugh outright. 'Did you feel rude?'

She shook her head, looked at Dacre for a thoughtful moment or two, then, claiming *him* this time as a member of her family, confided, 'From one family member to another, I think I can tell you that I believed Monsieur Gramache had it in mind to have a little flirt with me—only—' she laughed this time; it was a self-conscious sound '—only, I don't know how to do it.'

She glanced across at Dacre, and at his stern expression felt the lightness of her mood disappear. 'Did you not have other men-friends before Marc?' he demanded—and she realised then that his stern expression stemmed from an annoyance that she, his cousin's widow, should be flirting with some other man—even though she hadn't been.

'No, I didn't,' she answered, and was awash with the guilt of all her daytime nightmares—she should never have married.

Dacre looked at her long, hard and, she thought, speculatively. Then, his expression clearing, he asked, 'Did you want to flirt with our friend, the vet?'

'Of course not!' she answered stiffly. And, with a spurt of temper she could not control, snapped, 'Why am I always confiding in you things I don't tell other people?'

He stared at her. Then he laughed, and she liked that about him, and immediately her temper cooled. She took two cups of coffee over to the table and he pulled a chair near to him for her to sit down.

'Perhaps—um—because I'm your—cousin?' he suggested.

'Yes, but...' She gave a shaky, shuddery, confused kind of sigh. 'Why you—and—and not Marc?' she asked, the question leaving her with difficulty.

'You didn't tell Marc of the emotional scars your father left on you?'

She wasn't aware that she had any emotional scars—save for her hatred of and disquiet about physical aggression, which she had in common with most other people, she would have thought. But it was only as she looked across at Dacre then that she began to wonder, Would she, like her twin, have grown more and more confident but for that traumatic and repressive incident with her father? Would she in fact, when she had left her teen years behind, have left her accursed shyness behind too?

She didn't think so, but it was also a fact that since coming here, since leaving her father's home a month ago, she was far less shy than she had been.

She came away from the complexity of her thoughts when Dacre, obviously thinking that he had given her long enough to answer, changed tack to enquire, still in that same quiet, unhurried voice, 'Your sister—she knew of the distress your father caused you when you were fifteen?'

'No one knew,' Josy answered, but felt able to explain, 'Belvia was doing exams at school—well, both of us were actually—but whereas I seemed able to hide anything that worried me Belvia used to shout out in her sleep when she was worried. She was going through a shouting patch when it happened, so there was no way my mother or I was going to add to her anxieties.'

'So you decided to keep it to yourselves?' he ascertained, paused, then asked, 'You never thought to tell her after your mother's death?'

'How could I? We both loved our mother dearly.'

'So—just as you had protected your mother that day, when you dived in between your parents, you protected your sister from knowing anything about it.'

'I couldn't tell her. It would have crucified Bel to know that my father had once—probably more than once, for all I know—physically assaulted our mother!'

'Instead, you let it crucify you,' Dacre commented gently. Josy didn't answer. She well remembered in the year that followed how she would hurry apprehensively home from school every day to check that her mother was all right. 'And after your mother's death you carried it alone—and couldn't even tell the man you married.'

She had thought he had forgotten his earlier question about her not telling Marc of her emotional scars. And only then did she realise the full tenacity of the man. She should have recognised it in the fact that he had waited months for her to come to France to look after his horses. She realised then that he had always intended to have an answer to that earlier question.

It irked her a little. 'No,' she replied shortly, 'I couldn't.'

'Why?'

Damn him and his quiet questions. She didn't want to answer. She wasn't going to answer. Indeed, she wasn't sure she knew the answer. She flicked a glance across to where he was tenaciously waiting and damned him again.

She thought about getting up, leaving him and going about her business, yet something stopped her. All at

once it seemed to her that she had made a habit of
turning away from the unpleasant things in life. But this
was her new life, and hadn't she felt better for telling
Dacre of her bullying father's actions that day?

'It all seemed so dreadful, so violent, so—sordid,' she
pushed out painfully. 'Marc and I—we had a quiet,
gentle relationship. We—' She stopped; she couldn't go
on. 'I don't want to talk about it!' she said sharply.

Abruptly she shot to her feet and took her cup and
saucer over to the sink. Ye gods, another five minutes
of this seemingly bland probing and Dacre would have
from her how her relationship with Marc had ended up
anything but quiet and gentle!

She jumped, startled when, having not heard Dacre
move, she suddenly felt a hand on her arm as he turned
her about.

'Don't be upset,' he requested kindly.

His face was close—too close to hers. She didn't want
to look into his eyes; she didn't want him looking into
hers; she didn't want him to see the guilt that surely must
be there.

'I'm not upset!' she lied, and, shrugging his hand from
her, she did what she should have done some minutes
ago. She marched out of there.

Dacre rode César a couple of times that weekend and,
keeping herself busy, Josy saw very little of him. She
felt quite relieved when he went back to Paris. With luck
he'd stay there next weekend and she would have a chance
to settle down again. In truth she was finding him most
unsettling.

She had Marc much on her mind in the week that
followed, and thanked his cousin not at all that he had
stirred her memories of her husband. When she awoke
on Friday, however, a sense of fairness awoke with her.

It would be their wedding anniversary two weeks today, and the day after—the anniversary of Marc's death— she would have him very much on her mind with or without Dacre's questions, she realised.

She was down in the stableyard when she heard the sound of a car and looked up to see Regis Gramache pulling up. Feeling a touch reluctant, because she wasn't totally comfortable in his company, she left what she was doing, and as he got out of his car and came towards her she met him halfway.

'I must have misunderstood you, *monsieur*,' she began to apologise. 'I didn't realise you would be coming to see Nina again.'

'Regis.' He reminded her of his first name when there was entirely no need. 'You did not misunderstand, Josy. I have not come to see either of the horses, but you.'

'Oh!' she exclaimed, and was stuck. Then, with relief, she saw Georges pedalling like fury down the path towards them.

'I came to ask if you would care to have dinner with me one evening?' he asked in careful English while beyond him she saw Georges get off his bicycle and pretend to do something with the back wheel. Oh, heavens, a straight no sounded a bit blunt and she could feel herself colouring up. 'I know you are a widow-lady now, but I know I could help you over your sad time,' Regis Gramache went on.

Really! There was arrogance—and arrogance. Dacre had it without conceit. But this man! 'Thank you,' she answered politely, 'but I prefer to take my meals at home.'

'You wish me to dine with you here?' he asked, and, niggled by him or not, Josy discovered that her confidence had grown and that she just had to laugh.

'I wish nothing of the sort, *monsieur*,' she replied, but her dignity was shot, though, amazingly, she found that she was the one in charge when she politely told him, 'Perhaps I may telephone you when I feel like entering back into the dining-out world?'

She wasn't sure that he fully understood what she meant, but she gathered he'd got the gist of it when, taking her right hand in his, and perhaps holding it a little longer than necessary, he shook hands with her. 'Until then, Josy,' he answered warmly, and went back to his car.

'*Café*, Georges?' she asked as they watched the car drive away. Had that been *her*? Had that truly been her? Had she really handled that situation which at one time would have caused her to die a thousand deaths?

Josy was feeling very much cheered when she awakened the next morning. She guessed it was a hangover from yesterday when she had dealt with the amorous vet, and when Georges, as if he had seen the vet's car, and in the absence of any other of her family being about, had chased down to the stables to watch over her.

She went down to the stables feeling very much warm and protected, and as if she truly was a member of Dacre's family. She heard a plane overhead and realised that, contrary to her opinion last weekend, she didn't mind if Dacre would be home this weekend. She was out riding Nina when her newly found sense of humour tickled her again. She didn't mind Dacre coming home! Grief, it was *his* home! He'd every right to be there.

He was in the paddock checking some fencing when she returned. He saw her and left what he was doing to come over. Josy quickly got down from Nina and stood waiting as he came over to her. Her heart ached peculiarly as she waited for him to kiss her cheeks in greeting, and she hoped that he would think the warm colour she felt storm to her face was merely from the exertions of her ride.

'Hello, cousin.' He smiled in greeting, his look taking in her large eyes, her warm colour.

'Hello, Dacre,' she answered, and although she was so used to him now, and so at ease with him that she had parted with one of her two deepest secrets, she suddenly felt astronomically shy. Oh, Lord, and she had thought that she was at last—at long, long last—growing out of it!

'Have you had a good week?' he asked, and while last Saturday she might have told him all about Regis Gramache's visit yesterday this Saturday she felt too constrained to do so. And in no way could she make him coffee and stay in the confines of the kitchenette and drink a cup with him.

'Very good,' she replied, adding hurriedly, not giving him chance to say another word, 'Would you excuse me? I w-want to check something with César.'

The fact that she seemed to have slipped back into the shy, stammering person she had been before bothered Josy, and she kept out of his way for the rest of the day. Good manners if nothing else, however, insisted that she join him for dinner that night.

Hoping to give her failing confidence a boost, Josy dressed with care that evening—and thought she espied an admiring glint in Dacre's glance as he pulled out her chair at the table for her.

However, she might not have been able to tell him that morning of Regis Gramache's visit, but there was nothing admiring in Dacre's look when, halfway through their starter, he revealed that somebody had.

'I heard the vet paid a call yesterday,' he commented conversationally, though there was something in his tone that warned her before she said anything that he was not best pleased about it.

'Oh, yes,' she answered non-committally, deciding that perhaps it might be best to keep her answers brief.

'He wasn't here long enough to check the horses, though.'

'He wasn't,' she agreed.

'Are you being deliberately obtuse?' he suddenly bit aggressively.

'You're obviously looking for a fight!' Josy retorted, surprised at herself.

Dacre seemed surprised too. He mastered his aggressiveness, anyhow, and more peacefully, if tautly, demanded, 'So tell me about it.'

For several seconds she stared mulishly at him. But was then weakened by the thought that he was after all Marc's cousin, and as such had taken it upon himself to see that she was looked out for.

'He came to see me.'

Whatever French expletive left Dacre she didn't understand it. She understood his English, though, when, switching rapidly to her language, and all aggressive again, he barked, 'He has the audacity to come courting you in my home?'

'Courting?' she exclaimed. 'Hardly that!'

'Tell me, then!' he commanded.

'He came to ask me out to dinner.'

'You're *not* going!' he thundered before she could blink.

'That's for *me* to decide!' she yelled back, and then suddenly collapsed into laughter.

'What's so funny?' her host icily wanted to know.

'You—me.' With difficulty she controlled herself. 'I'm sorry, Dacre. I've never been like this with anyone.' His icy look started to thaw. 'We have a saying in England, "wouldn't say boo to a goose", and I've always thought that about summed me up. But here I am—not for the first time, if I remember rightly—yelling my head off at you. I confess,' she added, her laughter now done with, 'that since coming here I hardly know myself.'

For long, long moments Dacre just sat and looked at her, and then, his fury gone, he commented quietly, 'Good.' Then Agathe came in.

Josy puzzled about that 'Good' during her waking hours. And it was as she was walking down to the stables on Sunday morning that she realised, on remembering the way she had been when Dacre had called at her home—why, almost eight months ago now!—that she had come a long way since then.

Then, much as she loved Hetty, she had been unable to face going up to the stables to see her. Dacre, within an hour, had changed that. Dacre had, in fact, been responsible for bringing about many changes in her life. But for him she might never have made the break from her home. She had, she realised, a lot to thank him for.

She was not, however, of a mind to thank him for anything at lunchtime when she joined him at the lunch table, and he growled, 'You'll be wearing yourself and the horses out if you exercise them much more.'

So sack me, she felt like retorting, but, since he wasn't really employing her, and since he might well say, What a good idea, she of previous small retaliation held her tongue. 'They thoroughly enjoy it,' she replied calmly; but was honest enough to face up to the fact that, because Dacre was home she had deliberately kept them out longer. Somehow, and she could not pinpoint why, something was urging her to stay out of his way.

'Did you want to ride César?' she enquired.

'No,' was the clipped reply.

'You didn't—want me for anything?' she was unwise enough to venture.

'Not a thing!' he retorted sharply, and she hated, hated, hated him! So, OK, she couldn't think of a thing he might have come down to the stables to see her about either, but he could have been a little less blunt with his 'Not a thing!' reply.

With scarcely a word being spoken between them throughout the rest of the meal it was only good manners which kept Josy in her seat. Mutiny such as she had never experienced before was playing havoc with her, and she could hardly wait for the meal to end so that she could leave the table and take herself off somewhere.

At last she put down her napkin and, since she didn't think she could very well get up and leave without another word, she pushed back from the table and offered a defiant, '*Should* you need me for anything I'll be out on either Nina or César!'

Hostilely they stared at each other, but when she saw a minuscule movement at the corner of his mouth, as though he was hard put to it not to laugh, she turned abruptly away and made quickly for the door.

To her astonishment, however, Dacre had left his seat too and was at the door before her. She halted; he was blocking her way. She looked at him mutinously, and felt not one iota less mutinous when he drawled, 'Since you obviously work, think and dream horses, I'll take you to a performance of the Cadre Noir next week.'

And if you think I'm to be mollified by that you can think again, she fumed. Arrogant swine! 'Actually,' she told him loftily, and with no little delight, 'I've already been.' And had her ears assaulted for her trouble.

'Who with?' he snarled aggressively.

'By myself!' she retorted angrily. 'And very good company I was too!' With that she pushed past him and went up to her room to change. And if he hadn't gleaned from that that she preferred her own company to his, then tough!

By the time she had cooled down enough to realise that there was absolutely no earthly reason why he should want to mollify her anyway Dacre had returned to Paris.

Josy spent Monday and Tuesday hoping that for the next four and a half months or so—when her six months would be up—he would stay there. She found him too disturbing, too annoying, and much too much *too* everything else.

She owned that she had never felt so confused—and it was getting worse. Her sleep patterns were shot, and with the anniversary so close, if she didn't have Dacre on her mind, she had Marc.

On Friday night she dreamt of them both, and on Saturday morning she got up feeling drained and exhausted, and bogged down by feelings of inadequacy at the fact that she had been unable to love Marc as a wife should.

Josy went to the stables hoping with all she had that she and Dacre wouldn't strike sparks off each other this weekend. She didn't think she could cope with that. Then she found that she didn't have to—because he didn't come home that weekend.

She found that she was listening for his plane, and for a while alternated between being glad that he wasn't coming home and regretful. He worked hard—must do— and must want and need space to unwind to relax.

Oh, grief, was he fed up with her being there? Josy spent a worried ten minutes fretting about it before it dawned on her that if Dacre did not want her there then, family or no, it wouldn't take him long to find her somewhere else to live, even if it meant making a flat over the stables—and that triggered off thoughts of Marc, and she wondered if she was going mad.

Just as she also wondered why when at the beginning of the week she had hoped Dacre would never come home she was now missing him. Of course I'm not missing him, she contradicted. Nor did she care a jot that just because he'd got something heavy going on in Paris—undoubtedly with some stunning-looking female—he couldn't be bothered to stretch out a hand to the phone to tell somebody that he wouldn't be home.

Josy felt more mixed up than ever as, the weekend over, Monday gave way to Tuesday. She was still sleeping badly, and fresh guilt over Marc had appeared to haunt her.

On Friday—her wedding anniversary—she awoke so distracted that she felt that she had to go and visit Marc's grave. She attended to the horses early and, turning them out into the paddock, went to find Georges. In fractured French, with accompanying hand signs, she asked him to keep an eye on her charges while she drove into Saumur. Tomorrow, early, before Dacre arrived—if indeed he intended coming home that weekend—she would drive to Nantes.

It did not take her long to purchase a map and she returned home to take it up to her room. She opened it out, and judged that the journey would take about two hours. But, while she could see no problem in getting to Nantes, since she could barely remember Marc's fu-

neral, let alone the place where he was laid to rest, she
realised she might have a problem from then on.

It was still early—not quite eleven in the morning—
when, leaving the map open on her bed, Josy decided
to go downstairs and check in the library to see if there
were any maps there that might give her more precise
details of the Nantes area.

Somehow, too, she realised as she left her room, she
was going to have to let Agathe know where she was
going tomorrow. She couldn't leave for the day without
telling her. Then she would have to arrange something
about the horses.

She was halfway down the stairs when the front door
opened and, causing her to blink and wonder if she had
missed a day somewhere, Dacre came in.

She had halted, as had he. Then she carried on walking
down the stairs just as Dacre, a weekend bag in hand,
moved towards her.

'I didn't hear your plane,' was the first thing that came
into her head as they met at the bottom of the stairs.

'How are you, Josy?' he enquired, dropping his bag
to the floor and taking a hold of her arms, his eyes scru-
tinising her face.

'Fine,' she lied, knowing that she looked drawn and
strained and, in fact, a wreck.

Dacre scrutinised her for a second longer, then the
phone rang near by. He did not go to answer it immediately but kissed her cheeks and, causing her to stand
motionless from the shock of it, she was sure that he
pressed his warm cheek against hers.

Josy was still standing motionless when he let go of
her and went to answer the phone. I've imagined it, she
thought, but promptly came away from her surprise

when she realised that Dacre, who had answered the phone in French, had switched to English.

'Josy is here now,' he advised, and the next moment he was holding out the phone to her.

Josy went forward and took the phone from him. 'Hello?' she enquired.

'Hello, love,' her sister answered, and suddenly Josy was fighting to hold back tears. 'Was that Dacre Banchereau?'

'Yes,' she answered, and hid her tears in a shy smile to him as he looked back before picking up his bag and starting up the stairs, clearly on his way to his room.

'He sounds nice,' Belvia commented.

'He is.'

'How's your weather?'

'Beautiful,' Josy answered, and felt tearful again when her dear sister, who needed no excuse to ring her, got down to the real reason for this particular call.

'Latham and I came back last night—from a few days away, actually—and I thought, if it's all right with you, that I'd come this afternoon and stay with you for a couple of days.'

Josy swallowed down a knot of emotion at her sister's thoughtfulness. She knew her twin well. What Belvia was really saying was, I know it's your wedding anniversary, and I know that it will be twelve months tomorrow that Marc died—and I'll be with you.

Her sister had been with her a year ago, and it had been her sister who had kept her from cracking up. And Josy felt that she had never loved Belvia more than she did then. But this was the first year of Bel's marriage too, and as Belvia loved Latham so much, and Latham absolutely adored Bel, it would be painful for the two to be apart and Josy could not let her sacrifice herself any more.

'Oh, Bel, I'd love you to come,' she answered, battling to keep emotional tears out of her voice, 'but I won't be here.'

'Where are you going?' Belvia wanted to know at once.

'To Nantes.'

'I'll come with you,' she promptly offered, and Josy fought with all she had to be strong.

'No,' she answered. 'I'm all right now—honestly I am.' And, although she would have dearly loved her sister's company, went on, 'If you wouldn't mind, Bel, I think I should like to go on my own.'

There was a small silence the other end, then Belvia, proving that she was as sensitive as ever, asked, 'You're sure, Jo?'

Josy was battling harder than ever to hold back tears when a few minutes later she put down the phone. And there was no way she wanted to go to the library to search for any detailed map. All she wanted to do was to get to her room.

Fearful that she might break down before she got there, Josy raced up the stairs, and reached the top just as the door to Dacre's room opened.

Swallowing convulsively, she went swiftly past him and into the privacy of her own room. Only it turned out to be not so private as she had thought, because before she could turn about and close the door Dacre, without stopping to knock, was there too.

'What's wrong, *chérie*?' he asked urgently.

'M-my sister, sh-she wanted to come and stay for a f-few days,' Josy stammered on a gasp of emotional breath, wiping desperately at a stray tear which had escaped her control.

Dacre came closer and caught hold of that hand. 'That's nothing to cry over, little one,' he murmured, leading her over to sit on the edge of the bed. 'Agathe will make up a room for her in no time.'

'Belvia isn't coming.'

'She's not?' he queried, sitting down on the bed beside her.

Josy shook her head. 'I told her not to. I couldn't let her. Oh, she's been so good—' She choked. 'You've no idea ... Yet, even though she's married herself now, and is so happy, she's remembered that it's a year ago today that Marc and I married. A year tomorrow that Marc...' She couldn't go on.

'Shh...' Dacre soothed, and, letting go of her hand, he placed an arm about her shoulders and quietly held her.

They sat like that for some seconds, then Josy gave a shaky sigh, and suddenly became aware that Dacre had an arm around her. Her heart started to jump about; she thought it was panic. She pulled away from him and left the bed.

'I ... I'm all right now,' she told him, and knew he didn't believe that for a minute when he looked at her long and hard.

His attention having been all on her, as he too stood up he half turned, and only then noticed the map spread out on the bed.

'Thinking of going somewhere?' he enquired evenly, evidence of where she might be intending to go spread out before him.

'I want to take some flowers to Marc,' Josy answered, and saw Dacre give a slight nod, though whether of approval or merely acknowledgment of what she wanted to do she couldn't tell.

She was left staring blankly at him for a moment or two, however, when he stated, 'I'll drive you.'

'I'm not going until tomorrow—and I can drive myself,' she declined.

'I don't think so,' he decided for her. And, when it looked as if she might object, added, 'Look at you, all huge-eyed from the stress you're under. Have you slept at all this week?' he demanded.

'I—I'm all right,' she replied, suddenly no longer feeling weepy, but starting to feel angry. My God, this man! 'I'm no longer the emotional wreck I was. I—'

'I know that!' he retorted. 'The change in you since that day I called at your home is quite dramatic. But,' he went on when she drew breath to try to interrupt, 'you still have some way to go. And whether you know it or not—and I know you're going to battle like hell to ensure that no one sees you in tears—I don't think tomorrow will pass without you feeling a little emotional. 'Which is why,' he ended, his mouth quirking up at the corners, 'for the sake of any of my fellow countrymen who might be out on the road tomorrow, I will drive.'

He had a point there, she supposed, refusing to smile. She guessed she would not be giving her driving her entire concentration. 'I want to be off early.' She tried for a small obstruction anyway.

'I'll fly you there if you like.'

'No, thank you,' she replied politely.

'We'll leave here at eight,' Dacre decreed, then gave her something else to think about when he added, 'I think Marc's parents would appreciate it if we called on them.'

In an instant any hostility she was feeling towards him disappeared. 'They know I'm here—in your home?' she gasped.

'They have known from the time you gave me a definite date for your arrival.'

'And they don't mind—about it being me who's come to look after your horses?'

'They're delighted that you agreed to come,' Dacre assured her. 'They saw how happy Marc was to be with you. How—' Abruptly he broke off as a gasp of pain she could not control escaped her. 'What have I said? What...?'

Josy swiftly turned her back on him. 'He...' she gasped, but she couldn't tell him. Guilt stormed through her—guilt that would not let her be. Desperately she strove to get herself together but, swallow down emotional tears though she might, they were again coming nearer and nearer to the surface, and she just had to confess. 'You know that battle you spoke of? Well, would you mind leaving—while...' she swallowed '...while I'm still winning?'

She heard Dacre move, but it was not to the door as she had hoped but over to her. She kept her back to him and felt him take a hold of her arms. However, he did not turn her to face him but, allowing her her pride, in case she had lost her battle and had tears on her face, he just held her quietly by her arms.

'You have needed this year to mourn, little Josy,' he told her softly. 'But after tomorrow, I think—for your own sake, and for the sake of your happy memories of Marc—you should try to live for yourself.' With that he placed a light kiss in her hair.

That kiss and what Dacre had said affected her deeply. She didn't panic at his kiss to her hair; she had no need to. It had been more reverential than anything else. And yet it disturbed her. As too did his remark that after tomorrow she should try to live for herself.

She wanted to do that; she really did. The only trouble was that she suddenly felt so confused; she didn't know where she was going, or wanted to go, or what she wanted to do—or anything else any more.

CHAPTER FIVE

JOSY owned to being in sombre mood when just after eight the following morning Dacre headed his car in the direction of Nantes. She had little to say, and the nearer they got to their destination, the further she shrank into herself.

'Perhaps this wasn't such a good idea,' Dacre commented when half an hour had passed with not so much as a word coming from her.

'I—need to... I want to go,' she answered, and with a great effort, aware that he had given Franck and Georges instructions about the horses, she forced some conversation. 'Nina and César will be all right, won't they?'

Dacre's answer was initially to touch her left hand resting in her lap in a reassuring gesture. 'Who do you think looked after them when you took so long to get here?' he asked lightly—and she really did like him.

They stopped on the way so that she could purchase some fresh flowers. Because Marc had liked yellow Josy bought yellow roses and mimosa, and a vase to put them in.

Dacre carried the vase when they left the car. She had been worried that she might not remember where Marc's grave was. But proving that while he had been unable to attend Marc's funeral Dacre had since paid his respects, he guided her straight to the well-kept grave.

Fresh flowers had already been laid there, so Josy guessed that his parents had been early that morning.

Save for going and filling the vase with water from a nearby tap, Dacre stayed with her while she arranged the roses and mimosa, and she was pleased to have him there. Just as, after some minutes of standing with her in silence at Marc's graveside, she appreciated his sensitivity when he walked back to the car, leaving her alone with her memories.

Josy was still racked by the guilt of her last memories, but she remembered how Dacre had referred to her happy memories of Marc. She choked on a dry sob but made herself remember those happier times. She remembered Marc's goodness, his gentleness, his winning way with horses. But most of all she remembered his shyness. It had been that shyness that had caused her to be drawn to him. Next to her sister he had been her best friend. Dear Marc, her best friend and ... Tears stung her eyes, but she was glad she had come.

She walked back to the car. Dacre was standing by it. And she was taken out of the solemnity of her thoughts when, before she could open the passenger door, he came round and halted her by placing a hand on each shoulder. She felt herself begin to tremble but, made by him to stand still, she raised her face and found herself looking into a pair of serious, steady grey eyes.

'What ...?' she questioned faintly.

'I have to tell you,' he began quietly, 'that my aunt and uncle were very comforted when I told them that you would be coming here today.'

'You rang them?'

He nodded. 'They've invited us to lunch.'

'Oh, Dacre,' she whispered, and pulled out of his hold. He had said something yesterday about calling on them — and if she thought about it she supposed it was better that he'd telephoned them in advance rather than they

should just drop in on them. But she didn't want to go—knew that she didn't—not back to that house where ...
She couldn't be that brave; she ... Her thoughts fractured again.

She was Monsieur and Madame Paumier's daughter-in-law—the wife, widow, of their only child. And, even if she didn't feel like their daughter-in-law, Dacre had said that they had been very comforted to know she would be there today. Oh ... was she to be forever a coward? 'I don't think I'm very hungry, but ...' She bravely agreed.

Dacre murmured something soft and warm-sounding in French which she didn't catch, and probably wouldn't have understood anyway if she had. Then he was assisting her into her car.

Monsieur and Madame Paumier greeted them most warmly. 'Oh, how pale you are!' Sylvie Paumier exclaimed, and enfolded her in her arms, as too did Philippe Paumier. In fact, Josy had more of a hug from her father-in-law than she had ever had from her own father.

Lunch was less of an ordeal than she had thought it would be, and Josy guessed she had Dacre to thank for the fact that, whenever Marc's name came up, he would steer the conversation to light anecdotes about him.

Both Marc's parents spoke English, though neither was as fluent as Dacre and sometimes got matters a little back to front, which left it to him to come in with a translation. He did so again when Philippe Paumier brought the subject of money up. As well as her feeling awkward about it, the more her father-in-law tried to explain how Marc had wanted things, the more confused Josy became.

'I'm sorry, I don't understand,' she confessed, starting to feel a little hot and bothered.

'Don't be embarrassed, little one,' Dacre bade her. 'It is just that my uncle, because of the language difference, wants to be sure that you understand Marc's wishes and, incidentally, theirs. They say you've written to their lawyer refusing the provision Marc willed to you and mailed to his lawyer the week before your marriage, but—'

'Please, I can't. I never knew Marc had money. And...' her voice wobbled a bit '... I can't take it.'

'We are upsetting you. Oh, please forgive us,' Madame Paumier rushed in—and Josy felt worse than ever. It was they who should forgive her!

Josy felt quite desperate on the drive home. It had been a mistake to go and visit Marc's parents. She had pretended that she wasn't upset, of course. Because of their kindness to her, because they were Marc's parents, she had to pretend. They were going through a bad enough time as it was, without them thinking that she had gone away feeling worse than when she had come.

It was a silent drive back to the outskirts of Saumur. On the way to Nantes she had tried to lighten up; on the way back she felt too down to try.

'Thank you for taking me today,' she politely thanked Dacre when he halted the car at his home. She got out of the car and found that he was there on the gravel drive with her.

'You have had a bad year, *ma chère*,' he commented as he looked down into her troubled and expressive face. 'But remember that from tomorrow you are going to live for you—and not in the past.' Unspeaking, she stared at him, and he stretched out a hand and gave her arm a little shake. 'You'll remember?' he insisted.

Josy opened her mouth, hesitated, then promised, 'I'll remember,' and turned about and went indoors, leaving him to garage the car.

She went wearily up to her room. She had promised to live for herself. But what did that mean? When she had first come here she had thought it a start to a new life—a new life which would begin in earnest when she returned to England and, taking Hetty with her, got herself a job. But the thought of leaving this lovely and tranquil spot to start her new life suddenly didn't seem to have any meaning either!

Josy saw little of Dacre on Sunday. She exercised Nina and he came down to the stables and took César out, and returned to Paris before lunch.

That evening, needing some occupation, she wrote to her father—not that she thought he'd be too interested in how she fared. But, duty done, she then wrote to Tracey at the stables, in the hope that she might reply and give her more detailed information about Hetty's day-to-day welfare than—if she caught her at a wrong moment—she might over the phone.

On Monday Belvia phoned, and Josy chatted to her for a good ten minutes. And after that the week progressed, and Josy began to grow more restless and fidgety than she had ever been. She was still plagued by guilt over Marc, but for the first time she began to acknowledge that, since she could do nothing about it, that guilt was just something she was going to have to learn to live with.

The odd thing was, however, that while she felt so restless during the day, at night she had started to sleep better.

She awoke on Saturday feeling at once refreshed, and at the same time, as she recalled that Dacre would soon be here, she began to feel totally mixed up.

I haven't got enough to do, that's my trouble, she mused as, full of energy, she got out of bed. She had thought once or twice lately of asking Georges if he wanted any help in the garden. But a combination of shyness and the fact that Georges kept the gardens immaculate without her help kept her silent. It was also a fact, though, that looking after Nina and César was very far from being a full-time job.

A short while later, showered and breakfasted, she made her way to the stables. Already the day was warming up. She decided against saddling up the horses and taking them out but instead fed them and turned them out into the paddock. There were a few jobs she could be getting on with, but for the moment she watched as they frisked to the tree-shaded side of their enclosed area. Only when she became aware that she was listening for the sound of a plane did she grow impatient with herself and go and do a few chores.

By lunchtime she had neither seen nor heard Dacre. So, she'd be dining on her own tonight, she thought. Well, that was OK by her. She hoped he enjoyed himself wherever he was.

Josy went to bed that night in a very mixed-up frame of mind. For while part of her had started to grow quite anxious in case Dacre was ill, or something of that nature, there was another part of her that said she didn't give a damn that some glamorous-looking female was keeping him in Paris that weekend.

On the following Wednesday she awakened and went to her window to see that an early morning mist had settled over the landscape. It had been like that yesterday. The mist didn't take long to clear, and by nine a sunny day shone from a beautiful blue sky with only the merest scratch of cloud. Already it was a steaming-hot day.

Since she didn't like the idea of leaving the horses in their stables all day, the best thing to do was to turn them out into their shady paddock.

That did not take very long, and by eleven, their stables spruce and ready for their return, Josy walked back to the house. She felt hot and sticky and headed straight for the shower. She was under it when such a weight of restlessness took her that she just knew that she could not spend the day idly.

She had been to the town of Saumur several times. It was quite close by. She decided that she needed to go farther afield and went looking for Agathe. '*Je suis* going to Angers, Agathe.' She smiled as she hoped to convey that she was going to Angers. '*J'ai déjeuner*, Angers,' she added, to let the housekeeper know she would have lunch out. 'Nina, César...' she began.

'Franck *ou* Georges.' Agathe understood at once and gave her shy smile, and Josy went to get her car out in the confident knowledge that Agathe would instruct either her husband or Georges to keep an eye on the horses.

A little over an hour later Josy reached the city of Angers, and, finding a car park without difficulty, she left her car and strolled about. But she had little thought as to what she was doing or where she was going. She felt lost and alone, and there was an empty sort of ache inside her—it had been there for a few days—though she was mystified to know what that ache was.

She ambled into the Habitat shop and had a look round, but there was such a restlessness inside her that she came out again and walked on.

This is ridiculous, she lectured herself, and, seeing a crêperie in the Rue des Poëliers, with chairs and tables outside, she made herself go and sit down. She didn't want very much to eat—a snack would do. She ordered a *galette aux tomates et fromage*, and while she was waiting for her tomato and cheese pancake to arrive she wondered about Dacre. Then, trying to think about something else, for Dacre had seemed to spend quite a lot of time in her head just lately, she concentrated her thoughts on Hetty. Then all at once she became aware that there was a shadow in front of her.

Expecting it to be the waitress, she looked up, and her mouth opened in astonishment. Dacre Banchereau was standing there! And, just like that, in that very moment, she knew staggeringly that she was in love with him!

Her heart pounded; there was a roaring in her ears. She did not merely like him, she loved him! She would have welcomed a faint. But she didn't faint, and since Dacre seemed content to stand there watching her open-mouthed expression she took it that it was up to her to say something.

'What are you doing here?' she gasped.

'About to join you for lunch,' he drawled, and, bending down, he kissed both her cheeks. Then, while she was still striving for normality—when she had an idea that nothing would be normal ever again—he calmly took the seat next to her and asked what she had ordered.

'Er—the cheese and tomato crêpe,' she answered, the empty ache that she had carried around with her since he had not come home last weekend suddenly, as if by magic, gone.

'We'll be starving by dinnertime but I'll have the same,' he remarked conspiratorially.

She smiled, wanted to laugh; she was happy just being with him. 'How are they managing in Paris without you?' she controlled herself to tease—and felt as startled by her comment as Dacre looked. Grief—when had she so far forgotten her shyness to be so light-hearted?

Whatever, suddenly Dacre grinned at her sauce. 'With difficulty,' he answered wickedly, and she couldn't help it—she just burst out laughing.

Then she saw that Dacre still had his gaze on her, and swiftly she controlled herself. 'Er—have you been home?' she enquired.

'Flew in a couple of hours ago,' he answered, and she quite desperately wanted to know how long he was staying. But she kept silent. 'Agathe mentioned you were visiting the city, and since I had an errand this way I thought I'd come and help my English cousin with the menu. But—I was too late.'

Oh, she loved him, she loved him, she loved him. She especially loved him in this mood. It seemed to match her own so exactly. 'Um—I hate to tell you this, but there was a translation in English.'

'You know,' he murmured conversationally, 'without too much assistance you could grow to be quite cheeky.' She grinned. He stared. And she wanted that this lunchtime should never end.

But end it did, as it had to, and Dacre walked with her to her car. 'See you at home,' she offered, feeling shy again but hoping that he didn't mind her calling his home her home.

Apparently he didn't, for he looked at her warmly. 'Till then,' he said softly, and kissed her gently on both cheeks, and then stood back.

'Bye,' she mumbled, and got into her car and turned the ignition. For the first few minutes of her journey she negotiated city traffic while at the same time wondering at the fact that, out of all the places she could have halted at to have a snack, she had chosen one on the route Dacre had been walking.

She had cleared the city traffic and was on a straight part of the road from Angers to Saumur when she had space to give most of her attention to the astonishing and unbelievable fact that she was head over heels in love with Dacre. She did not have to dissect it. It was just there. She loved him—and it was like no other feeling she had ever known.

Quite when on that journey back to Dacre's home her feeling of inner happiness began to fade she could not have said. All she knew by the time she halted her car was that there was going to be very little joy for her in this love for Dacre that had come uninvited and unasked for.

Josy left her car on the front drive and, feeling all over the place suddenly, got out, leaving it where it was, and, feeling in the need of some action, took a walk down to the paddock.

Nina and César trotted over to her, and she crooned to them for a while, then fell again to thinking of the love she had for Dacre, which was still there—this different kind of love—and which, she just knew, always would be there.

She had loved Marc, but not in this way. But, while admittedly the love she had had for Marc had been nothing like this all-encompassing love she felt for Dacre, she faced the fact that she should never love any man. She had loved Marc—and he had died.

Josy was standing by the paddock rail, deep in thought while trying to find peace of mind, when suddenly Dacre came striding towards her. She felt immediately jumpy. Oh, how dear he was; how she loved him—but oh, how she should not. Pain smote her, and as he drew level and halted she looked away.

If he had expected to see his laughing companion of lunchtime, or the shy but happy woman he had parted from in the car park, then it was patently obvious his expectation would come to nought.

Silently he studied her. 'What's wrong, Josy?' he asked abruptly, his glance fixed on her lifeless expression.

Her heart thudded painfully, and she felt that she would just about die if ever he had so much as the merest inkling of how she felt about him. 'Nothing,' she answered woodenly—and too late saw that she should have known him better than to think he would let her get away with that.

'Don't lie to me!' he objected sternly.

'I'm not lying!'

'Something's upsetting you!' He let go something angry-sounding in French, then calmed down to ask, 'What is it? In Angers you were—'

'We're not in Angers now!'

'You're unhappy here, then?'

'Of course not!' she flew at him, starting to grow angry herself. 'I love it here—you must know that I do.'

'So what happened between here and Angers?' he was back to demanding to know.

'I don't need this!' she exclaimed hotly, and went to turn away from him but, tenacious as she had known he would be, he wasn't letting her get away with that either.

'Will you stop trying to hide from matters that bother you?' he roared, catching hold of her right arm and swinging her back to face him.

'Take your hands off me!' she shrieked.

'Then tell me what's wrong!'

She'd die sooner. 'Why do you want to know?' she yelled, her panic momentarily clearing, allowing her to see that her only way out lay in attack.

'So there *is* something!' he exclaimed triumphantly, and, loving him, she wanted to hit him.

Furiously she pushed him away. His eyes glinted; he didn't like it. 'What do you want from me?' she cried in anguish.

And she nearly dropped when, his anger with her out of control, he bellowed, 'I want you to marry me!'

'No!' she gasped, horrified, her breath sucked in; he looked as shaken that he had actually said those words as she felt to have heard them.

He recovered first, however. 'The idea's so alien to you?' he asked toughly, the fact that she was horror-struck not lost on him. 'The idea of being my wife, the mother of my children—'

'*Stop*!' she screamed. 'Don't...' She couldn't take any more, but turned and ran from him. This time, perhaps because he judged it would do more harm than good to try to hold on to her a second time, he let her go.

Josy was still in a state of shock when an age later she came to to realise that she was sitting in an armchair in her bedroom but could not remember how she had got there.

What she could remember, however, was that Dacre had clearly stated, loudly enough for anyone around to hear, that he wanted her to marry him. Stars above! But, worse, he had spoken of children, so he wasn't interested in a 'name only' type of marriage. And, remembering the virile look of him, she wouldn't have believed him if he'd said he was.

A shaky fifteen minutes later everything was still whirling around in her head. Dacre had said nothing about love—perhaps he didn't think that love was necessary. His attitude would be just a convenient, I'll be home at the weekend—mostly. Occasionally in the week too. You just look after the horses—the babies too when they arrive. Oh, God, she felt she really was going mad. Babies! Heaven help her—she couldn't bear that any man should touch her!

Josy was dragged out of the agony of her thoughts when someone knocked at her bedroom door. She started nervously, and then decided, since Dacre was more likely to walk straight in than knock and wait, that it must be Agathe.

She went and opened it—but it was Dacre. He was serious-faced, watchful. 'Are you all right?' he wanted to know.

Cracking up fast, she could have told him. 'Fine,' she replied stiffly.

'You look dreadful,' he informed her. She wanted to say, Thanks, but nothing would come out. 'Try to rest in between now and dinner,' he suggested, not unkindly.

'I—' she began, on the way to telling him that she would be giving dinner a miss that night.

'And after dinner we'll talk, you and I,' he cut in to decree.

She didn't want to talk to him either. As she saw it there was nothing to talk about. She had covered all that needed to be discussed in that horrified, No, she had given him in reply to his suggestion that she marry him.

Then she recalled his accusation that she tried to hide from matters. 'Yes,' she confirmed reluctantly.

He nodded. 'Try to rest,' he repeated, and walked away.

Josy went slowly back into her room. She caught sight of her face in the mirror. It was ashen. She decided, regardless of his repeated instructions to rest, that she'd had enough of her room.

Belatedly she remembered that her car was still parked out front. She left her room, but when she went out through the front door her car was not there. Dacre, she realised, must have garaged it for her.

She felt better for being outside, she realised, and un-hurriedly walked down to the stables. It was early evening by that time, but Georges, working overtime as he some-times did, was down there making a fuss of both her charges. She waved to him and he indicated that he would put Nina and César to bed for the night.

Josy walked back to the house, reflecting that it had been kind of Dacre to garage her car, kind of him to come to her room and check that she was all right, while at the same time she was fast regretting that she had agreed to have a talk with him after dinner.

What good would talking do? It wasn't as though he loved her; he would laugh his French socks off at any ridiculous notion that his reason for wanting to marry her was anything more than expediency. He had decided that it was time he did something about having a wife and children and she—already installed in his home—was trustworthy and already family too. What could be more convenient, more efficient?

She couldn't be sure that that was the way his thoughts went, of course. And since being here she had grown stronger than she had been, and in his home she had been happier than she had ever expected to be again. And, not least because she loved him and because of his kindness, she owned that she owed him more than a horrified, No, by way of explanation for why she would not marry him.

In her room she showered and changed, but the closer it got to eight o'clock, the less she felt like eating, or seeing Dacre again. She had no idea what explanation she could possibly give him.

But, as panic began to bite at some unwanted honesty within her that decreed she must either face him or return to England, so her watch showed eight. And because she loved him, and wanted to stay here with him, she found the courage to go down the stairs.

At the sound of her footsteps Dacre came from the open *salon* door, and, while she somehow managed to keep walking towards him, inside she froze.

'Shall we go and see what delicious morsels Agathe has prepared for us tonight?' Dacre offered.

Josy went with him to the dining-room. If that had been his way of easing a taut situation, he need not have bothered. She wanted to run; she shouldn't have come down. Oh, why, oh, why had Dacre had to complicate what—up until this afternoon—had been a wonderful arrangement?

She took her usual seat in the dining-room, but Agathe could have placed a dish of chaff before her for all she was able to enjoy the housekeeper's superb cooking. She felt apprehensive, on edge, and, while she didn't want any sort of conversation with Dacre, she wanted anything that had to be said over and done with so that she could go back to her room.

She barely touched her first course. She tried hard with her second course, but found that to swallow anything at all took a tremendous effort, and she jumped, startled, when Dacre said suddenly, 'Relax, Josy.' And she saw it was as futile to deny that she felt jumpy. She saw his glance go to her plate, and found her voice.

'W-would you apologise to Agathe for me, and—and tell her that I had a big meal at lunchtime?' she asked.

'*Certainement*,' he replied urbanely, having seen for himself just how much she had eaten at lunchtime and yet not batting an eyelid at her lie. 'Would you care for some wine?' he enquired.

'No, thank you,' she returned politely; he might think it would help her to relax, but she was more interested in keeping a clear head.

She was surprised none the less when, his meal not finished either, he all at once stood up. 'My dear, you look just as if you're waiting for Madame Guillotine. Shall we go and get this over?'

'Your dinner?' she protested, again wanting to run.

'Come.' He refused to prevaricate, and came round to her chair. Josy moved before he reached her and they went from the dining-room to the *salon*.

Josy moved further into the room. She wanted this over in two minutes flat. But when Dacre closed the door and indicated that she take a seat she knew it was not going to be that quick—or simple.

Yet as she sat down, and Dacre took a chair facing her and her apprehension deepened, so she determined that it *was* that simple—of course it was. If she wanted this over quickly then, since Dacre was saying nothing, it was up to her to get started—and finished.

She looked up to see that he was eyeing her steadily, took a deep breath and, on a panicking instant of courage, started off. 'I'm sorry if my...' words failed her for a moment '...my—if the way I said no this

afternoon was a bit abrupt. What I should have said—
well, fr-frankly—I was a bit—er—taken aback by your
prop—by what you said—was that I'm afraid I can't—
um—marry you b-because I shall never marry again.'

There, it was said! And if Dacre was anywhere near
as kind as she thought him he would let her return to
her room without further argument. Josy started to
breathe a trace more easily, and even put her hands on
the arms of her chair prior to getting up. But then it was
that she discovered that he wasn't so kind as she had
believed—and that he *did* want further explanation!

'It's not—just me?' he enquired quietly.

Dear God, she loved him! If anyone, it would be him.
'No,' she answered.

'Then why, Josy,' he wanted to know, 'do you think
you will never marry again?'

She stared at him—and would not answer. Nor could
he make her answer. There seemed to be a determined
kind of glint in his grey eyes—as if he knew that it was
more than that she felt it would be a betrayal of Marc,
of her love for her dead husband, if she married again—
and determinedly Dacre was waiting. But she could be
determined too.

Dacre waited silently, not moving but patiently re-
solved that she should answer his question. She started
to feel jumpy again, and flicked a nervous glance to the
door. Then she looked back at him. His gaze seemed to
have softened, and she loved him, and although what
she truly wanted to do was run, somehow—perhaps because of what he had said to her about hiding away from
things, or perhaps because her love for him was weak-
ening her—she found that she could not run.

Nor could she sit still either. She got up from her chair,
and Dacre rose too—though whether from politeness or

in order to be at the door before her if she made a run
for it she could not tell.

She did not make for the door, however, but turned
to walk over to the windows. It was still light enough to
see out, but she saw nothing of the view as she fought
for composure to tell him what he insisted on knowing—
what she had never told another living soul.

'Is it so painful, my dear?'

She had not known that he was so close. She turned.
Oh, Dacre, she mourned silently, you've no idea.

'Yes,' she owned, even at that late stage hoping he
would let her off the hook. But he didn't, and while she
again toyed with the idea of trying to leave the room she
realised that because she loved him and because he had,
in a manner of speaking, proposed, she owed him more
than that.

'You said—accused...' she began, made a faulty start,
and began again. 'This afternoon you accused me of
trying to hide from things that bothered me. Well...'
she paused to take a shaky but controlling breath '...well,
that's not true. You're wrong,' she managed.

'Come and sit down,' Dacre suggested, his voice quiet,
his tone hypnotic—so much so that she allowed him to
lead her over to a sofa, where he sat down with her and,
turning to her, prompted softly, 'Go on. Tell me how
I'm wrong.'

She looked at him and away again, could not bear to
see the look in his eyes change. And after another shaky
start she began, 'I've hidden from nothing, Dacre.
Ever—ever—since Marc died I've been crucified by
facing up to the... guilt that is mine, the guilt that I was
to blame for—his accident, the guilt for...' her voice
started to fade '...for his death,' she ended on a
hushed sound.

She couldn't look at him. She didn't want to look at him, to see hate and loathing in his face that she had been responsible for the death of someone loved and of his family. She moved to get up—and found his hand had come to her arm as he held her still.

Then his other hand was coming beneath her chin, and he was forcing her head up, forcing her to look up into his eyes. She looked, studied those grey eyes so close, but—unbelievably—saw not a hint of hate.

'Marc was thrown from his horse, Josy,' Dacre stated quietly.

'No,' she denied, then changed it to agree, 'Well, he fell; y-yes, he did. But it was because of—m-me. Because I . . .' Her voice faded; she couldn't tell him that—nothing on this earth would make her. 'He wasn't thinking what he was doing. When he fell off Diamant he wasn't thinking what he was doing. We'd . . .' She couldn't go on.

Then she found that she didn't need to, for, looking absolutely thunderstruck, something pretty explosive in French was leaving him. 'Oh, my dear, dear Josy—have you thought for all this while that Marc's death was your doing?' Dacre questioned. And while she stared at him, a mass of agitation, yet with a heart that pounded to hear him call her 'My dear, dear Josy', he said, 'Did no one tell you—?' He broke off, totally incredulous.

'Tell me what?' she asked, but was too het up to wait for an answer as she rapidly explained, 'W-we were all in shock—upset. I know I wasn't taking very much in— any conversation was all in French anyhow. But I don't remember much of anything, save that Belvia—who knows about as much French as I do—was there. All I could think, and know, was that if I'd acted differently then Marc would not have been upset—and that made me responsible for him falling off Diamant.' She gave a shuddery, racked kind of sigh—and became aware that Dacre had his hands on her shoulders, and was giving her a little shake.

She looked at him, saw that his expression was stern, and could not bear his hatred of her for her part in Marc's death. But she was then snapped out of her emotional unhappiness when, giving her shoulders another small shake, he bade her urgently, 'Listen to me, Josy, and hear every word. You were *not* in any way, shape or form responsible for my cousin's death.'

'I was.' She refused to believe him. 'Marc fell off—'

'Marc couldn't have fallen off a horse if he'd tried,' he contradicted her. 'He was born knowing how to ride. He did it instinctively; he didn't have to think about it— it was second nature to him.'

'Yes, but—'

'From a very early age his father would just sit him on a pony and Marc and pony were as one.'

'But—'

'Josy, Josy, hear me,' Dacre cut in, and, pausing for a moment, an alert look there in his eyes, he went on, 'You were obviously having—um—honeymoon problems.' She coloured, but somehow managed to keep eye contact. 'But, believe me, that had nothing to do with the fact that that black-hearted stallion threw him.'

Her eyes widened. She didn't believe their 'honeymoon problems', as he'd put it, had had nothing to do with it. But this was the first time she'd heard that Marc had been thrown! 'Threw him?' she questioned.

'That's what I said. Nor was it the first time.'

'It wasn't?'

His answer was to stare at her stunned. 'Didn't Marc tell you?' he asked.

She shook her head. 'He never mentioned it. What happened? Was he hurt?'

'He was in hospital for weeks—months,' Dacre replied, and, his look on her softening, he went on, 'Oncle Philippe was determined to have Diamant put down then, but Marc wouldn't hear of it. He wouldn't believe the brute had bad blood. So my uncle stabled him while Marc recovered and went on a European convalescent trip.'

'He was still convalescing when he found work at the stables?' Josy questioned; there was so much she hadn't known about Marc—his accident, his wealth. 'But he had no need to work!' she exclaimed.

'He wouldn't have called it work. In all probability he refused payment. But it would have been natural to him to head for the nearest stables.'

'His accident with Diamant wouldn't have put him off,' she stated, remembering Marc's love of horses.

'It wouldn't have,' he agreed. 'Just as, when he returned to his French home, his parents knew that within twenty-four hours Marc would be risking his neck on that devil stallion again.'

'And Diamant threw him again?' she questioned.

'He did. Despite his father warning him, Marc couldn't wait. They went towards the woods...'

'I was with him.' Josy, hardly aware that she had spoken, took over. 'Marc took off at a gallop—and I lost sight of him.'

'They were in the woods when the stallion made up his mind that he didn't want anyone on his back. One of the estate workers was there when he saw the beast rearing and bucking—even an expert like Marc was having difficulty hanging on. Marc was killed when the horse forcefully slammed him into a low-branched, solid tree.'

Josy stared at him, wanting to believe that Marc being thrown had had nothing to do with her. But, having gone through a whole year of dreadfully disabling guilt, she was finding it difficult to believe totally.

'You're sure?' she questioned.

'Absolutely positive,' Dacre answered unhesitatingly. 'I went to see Émile Caillère—the estate worker—myself a few weeks after it happened.'

'Oh—Dacre!' she exclaimed tremulously; could she let go of this dreadful guilt? Dared she let go? Dacre didn't know about... But...

'Oh—Josy,' he breathed softly, in return. 'I am so sorry that on top of losing Marc you have so suffered by thinking you were to blame.'

From somewhere she found a smile—a watery kind of smile. In a moment she would go to her room and digest all that he had said. But first she just had to stay and say, 'Thank you, Dacre. Thank you for telling me all you have.'

'You should have been told before. It should never have been left this long,' he stated, adding, 'I can only assume that my aunt thought the deep shock you were in came from the fact that you had not only lost Marc but had been a witness to his accident.'

'That must have been it,' she agreed, and was ready to return to her room. 'Thank you again,' she murmured, her head crammed with all he had revealed, hope starting to break through. Dacre had sounded so certain. Could it really be as he'd said, that Marc's accident was totally unconnected with their 'honeymoon problems'? 'I think I'll—er—say goodnight now, and...'

She halted when once more he stretched out a hand to stay her. She looked up, startled, and was shaken to see that that look of determination was back in his eyes. 'We haven't had our discussion yet,' he reminded her.

'We've been talking for the last ten minutes!' she protested.

'We've been talking about a side-issue that came up—something you should have known about a year ago, and which just had to be cleared away—cleared from your conscience before we went any further.' He corrected any misapprehension she might be under that he was in any way satisfied with her reasons for stating that she would never marry again.

'I—you . . .' she choked. And when she could not go on she discovered that he could and—what was more—that once he and his tenacity got hooked into something there was not the smallest glimmer of a chance that he would let go.

'To return to the reason why you thought Marc was not concentrating on his riding,' he took up conversationally. 'The honeymoon problems you were having.' She stared at him as if hypnotised, and just could not believe it when, his hands coming to her arms just as if he was aware that she might at any moment bolt, he asked very quietly, 'Tell me, Josy, did you ever make love with him?'

Stupefied, she stared into his steady grey eyes, his question rioting around in her head. Disbelieving, she stared—and still couldn't believe that she had heard what she had heard. And then she came to a very rapid decision—she was getting out of here! Her defences, admittedly, were down, but no way was she going to talk to him about *that*!

CHAPTER SIX

JOSY did not make it as far as the door. As if suspecting
that she would take off, Dacre was ready for her and
held firmly on to her as she leapt from the sofa.

'Let me go!' she shrieked, panicking wildly.

'Shh—I'm not going to hurt you,' he gentled her,
keeping her at arm's length, but his hold unbreakable.
'You've been very brave, but there are still matters to
be aired—matters to be faced.'

'I've faced them all—and they're nothing to do with
you!' she hurled at him furiously. This man—he made
her *so* angry! So... So...

'I don't agree. They have everything to do with me,'
he countered.

How he came to think that whether or not she had
made love with his cousin was anything to do with him
she failed to see. She fought desperately for calm but
hurled at him heatedly, 'My bedroom secrets are my
own!'

'Normally I'd say you were right, and that my question
was a gross impertinence. But nothing is normal here
and...' he hesitated '... and I think it's important to us
that we have this—discussion.'

She felt panicky again. She didn't like that word 'us'.
But with a great effort she managed to hold down her
panic, and since she didn't like Dacre holding her, and
since it did not seem as if he was going to let her out of
the room in a hurry, she took a step towards the sofa,
and he let her go.

Only when she was sitting down did he go and take the chair opposite. Josy did not look at him. She was his prisoner; he could do his worst, but not another peep was he getting out of her!

For long, long, tortured seconds she was aware of Dacre looking at her. Stubbornly she showed him her profile. A taut silence stretched, and strained seconds ticked away. And still she would not look at him.

That was until quietly, gently into that silence, Dacre answered his own question. 'I don't believe you did make love with him on your honeymoon night, little one.' And then he added, 'Nor do I think you gave yourself to my cousin—or to any man—before your marriage.'

Josy turned her head. Dacre's look was as quiet as his words. 'Th-that's still got nothing to do with you!' she exploded shakily, her eyes measuring, hopelessly, the distance of her sofa from the door in relation to his chair and capture.

'Oh, little virgin, I'm not blaming you,' he breathed softly, seeming to know for a fact from her answer that she was indeed a virgin. And that, combined with her guilt, rattled her into being unwary.

'Then you should!' she erupted.

'I should?' he enquired, his tone mild—whereas she was going out of control.

'Yes, you should!' she retorted agitatedly. 'I should never have married Marc! I wanted to live with him, but not as a wife.' Horrified at what she had just confessed, Josy stared at Dacre, unable to believe that he had goaded her to reveal that. She had no idea how she had expected him to look, but to her surprise, save for a steady sort of waiting look in his eyes, Dacre still wore the same quiet expression. 'You're—not angry?' she asked.

'I'm not angry,' he confirmed, and asked, 'Did you not love him?'

'Yes, of course I loved him!' she stated unequivocally. 'Next to my sister Marc was my best friend.'

'You loved him as a good friend—and not as a husband?'

'Welcome to my nightmare!' she invited, no longer wondering about the various emotions Dacre provoked in her—some so violent that they sent shyness flying. She was in love with him—and he and it had turned her world upside-down.

'So tell me about your nightmare,' he invited in turn. 'When did it begin?'

Josy stared at him. That was something she hadn't been prepared to share with anyone—not even Belvia—so why were words bubbling up inside her? She loved Dacre, yes, but he wasn't her best friend.

'Marc was my very good friend.' She was barely aware that she had spoken. 'I never felt threatened by him.' She didn't seem able to stop. 'Somehow it seemed that he was more shy of me than I was of him.'

'So, recognising his shyness, you spoke to him to try and make him feel more comfortable, more at ease in your country?' he suggested, surprising her that he seemed to know how it had begun.

'I—er—yes,' she admitted, and found herself going on, 'And, crazy though it now seems, we somehow got married without—er—passion entering into it.'

'You had a passionless engagement.'

'Well, we were only engaged for a month, and there was a lot to see to—getting the flat ready and everything.' She halted. 'Why am I telling you all this?'

He looked levelly back at her. 'Because it's important that you should,' he stated, and, perhaps because she did love him so much, as she stared at him Josy found that she trusted him to be right. 'So, feeling unthreatened by Marc, you married him expecting a passionless marriage, and—'

'I didn't even think about it that deeply. I told you, we were friends! We had a mutual love of horses; I just didn't think about anything else.' A shaky breath escaped her. 'But,' she added, 'I should have done.'

'You didn't think about the physical side of marriage?'

'It wasn't an issue,' she replied, her voice growing shaky as she remembered how it had been. 'I suppose, if anything, I just assumed—Marc and me being such good friends and everything—that everything would sort itself out—' She broke off, unable to go on.

'Take your time, *petite*,' Dacre encouraged.

'There's nothing more to say,' she replied in a whisper of a voice. 'Marc and I came to his parents after the marriage ceremony—and my life became a living nightmare from that day on.' Her voice faded away; she had nothing more to add and silence filled the room once more. She thought Dacre made a movement as though he would have come over to her—but something caused him to hold back.

But he did not hold back from wanting to find out more, however, and there was a deep sincerity there in his voice when he said, 'Josy, my dear, please believe that I am not merely prying for the sake of it when I tell you that I need to share more of that nightmare with you.'

'You don't!' she retorted, getting angry again. What did he want—blood? 'We married, and Marc became a stranger to me—how do you like that?' she snapped. 'I knew him as a quiet, shy, gentle person, and yet there he was—th-that night—a stranger. An aggressive stranger. T-tearing at my clothes!' she cried, distraught. 'Throwing m-me on the bed. Aggressive, brutal—I was terrified!'

'Oh...' In an instant Dacre was over by her side, on the sofa with her, an arm coming round her.

'*No*!' she hurled at him, angry, agitated, and barely knowing how much she'd revealed, how much she had kept to herself, pushing him away from her. 'You want to hear the rest of my nightmare—the months of torment I've gone through in coming to terms with my inadequacies, my frigidity that caused a man to ride into the woods the next day and get killed?'

'M—'

'*No*!' she raged. This had been pent up inside her for too long. He wanted to hear it—let him; perhaps then she wouldn't hurt so much. 'You want to hear how that night, our wedding night, Marc slept in the dressing-room while I—chaste in my bed, and glad, oh, so glad of it—wondered what on earth I was doing there, why on earth I had married Marc?'

'You—'

She refused to let him get in. 'That night, and every night since, especially in those early months that followed, I've lain awake wondering why I married Marc at all. Wanting to live with a beloved good friend no longer seems sufficient reason. So was it more that with sweet, kind, gentle Marc sounding me out about marriage, I saw it as the tailor-made excuse I needed for leaving home? 'My sister was still there, but I'd sensed that she was only staying because of me, that I was holding her back—that once I'd gone she wouldn't hang around and put up with any nonsense from my father. So did I marry Marc merely to escape—only to find myself in a worse situation?'

'You bore all these nightmarish thoughts alone?'

'Who would I have told?' she charged.

'Your sister?'

'Have you *no* idea how I felt?' she exclaimed, her voice trembling in her agitation. 'Can you imagine what it feels like to face up to the fact that you're passionless, that you don't want passion, that you're cold to it? I froze that night! Have you any idea how I felt after what I'd done to Marc, and—because I'd as good as caused his death—how I needed to feel? How could I have confessed any of it to Belvia?' she hurtled on. 'I know her; we're twins—she would have found excuses for me. I didn't want excuses. I hurt, and it was right that I should hurt. But for me, Marc would be alive. Oh, I was so unfair to him!' she cried in an agony of distress—and did not know that Dacre had both her hands in his until he gripped them tightly.

'Shh...' he tried to calm her. 'Oh, Josy, Josy, little one, you've been in hell,' he murmured softly, and gave her hands a little shake, as if to get her full attention. She looked at him, all large eyes and ashamed, and, having got her attention, 'Josy, my dear, listen to me,' he urged, and when, suddenly feeling too exhausted to move, she just sat and stared at him, he stated, in a tone that brooked no arguing, 'It was not you who was unfair to Marc, but Marc who was unfair to you.'

Josy did not believe that. 'That's not true!' she argued bluntly.

But Dacre was not backing down and, with his grey eyes holding hers, suggested, 'There were a lot of things Marc didn't tell you—I think you'll agree?'

'I—didn't know he had a—moneyed background, if that's what you're referring to,' she answered, calmer now, if still inwardly trembling after her emotional outburst. 'And I'd like my hands back, please,' she added crisply, not sure that she liked this tough, let's-dig-out-the-truth man, after all.

'Nor did you know of the various properties he owned—some of which he willed to you,' Dacre informed her, letting go of her hands.

'He was a property owner?' she enquired, thereby unwittingly revealing something else she hadn't known.

'Nor did you know about his accident,' he went on.

'Not until you told me about it,' she agreed, and was in no way prepared for what was coming when, his grey-eyed look steady on hers, he set about proving that Marc had been unfair to her.

'So, since Marc could not have told you the result of that accident without revealing he'd had an accident,' Dacre resumed, 'I think it's safe to say that you had no idea that the accident left Marc—impotent.'

'Impotent!' she exclaimed, warm colour coming to her face.

'I'm afraid so,' he confirmed, trailing the backs of the fingers of one hand down the side of her flushed cheek. Hurriedly Josy pulled back.

'I don't bel… How—?' No, not how. It wouldn't mean very much to her if he went into detail. 'I can't believe you!' she stated immovably. 'That night—the night of our marriage—he came after me like someone demented!'

'My dear, my poor dear, if you knew more of men you might—' Dacre broke off, but went on to expound, 'From what you've said, I'm fairly certain that my cousin, realising certain duties were expected of him that night, forced himself to be aggressive in the belief that aggression might push him through the barrier of his impotency.'

'No!' she gasped faintly. 'I...' She still couldn't believe it. But, her head in an emotional whirl from all she had said and from what Dacre had revealed, she suddenly remembered something—and didn't believe him at all. 'You once asked me if I was pregnant!' she challenged, hitting his lies about Marc being impotent soundly on the head—but only to find that Dacre had an answer for that too.

'It was soon after his accident, while he was still in hospital, that Marc told me the result of that stalliion half killing him. I could only assume, when I met you and Marc said you were married, that the surgeons who repaired him had been mistaken in their diagnosis. 'Forgive me, *ma chère*—Marc was twenty-five when you married and, for all his reserve, he'd had an affair or two. And you, little one—so beautiful, so shy—are a very desirable woman.'

Her heart fluttered to hear Dacre say that she was beautiful, but while she wanted him to think her beautiful she didn't want him thinking her desirable. 'What's the way I look got to do with anything?' she questioned— a tinge belligerently, she had to admit.

'You're lovely, and so unworldly,' he replied, which in her view was no kind of answer. 'Whether the medical people were right or wrong, I knew in that moment of meeting you—without actually thinking about it—that if it was possible for any woman to restore Marc's manhood then you could—or maybe had. But a short while ago you confirmed that you had not, and I knew that the surgeons who put him back together again had been right—Marc was impotent.'

'You... He... Oh, Marc, poor Marc,' she mourned—and that night she had screamed in terror!

'Poor Josy,' Dacre corrected her softly. 'You went through all—'

'Did his parents know?' she asked, remembering how she and Marc, avoiding eye contact, had gone down to the stables without seeing either his mother or father the next morning. 'About Marc...'

He shook his head. 'He couldn't talk to either of them about it. I was more of an older brother he was able to confide in.'

'And... you're sure?' she asked.

'I'm sure,' he answered steadily. 'But if you, as Marc's widow, would like a medical report, it would be no problem for me to arrange confirmation for you.'

Josy gave a shaky sigh—and realised that she believed him, and had for a few minutes believed him. 'That won't be necessary,' she said quietly, and then, silently owning to feeling very mixed up about absolutely everything and needing very much to be alone so that she could sort out her head, she asked, 'Do you want me to go back to England?' Somehow, confusingly, it seemed that she had just cut all ties as a family member.

She was relieved, though, when she saw a slow smile come to Dacre's face. From that smile she gathered that he would not be throwing her out come morning. Her relief, however, was short-lived, and she gasped in shock when he answered gently, 'Oh, no, *chérie*, I want you to stay here in France—and marry me.'

Josy felt the colour rush to her face and then drain away, and she stared at him in stunned amazement. 'Haven't you been listening to anything I've said?' she exclaimed.

'I've heard every word,' he replied, calm where she was all agitation again.

'Then you *know* I can't marry you!' she erupted, on her feet and in panic. 'I can't be a wife—to any man! It wasn't only Marc who c— It was me too!' Dacre had risen as well, but while she was panicking wildly she saw that his glance was as steady as ever.

Dearly did she want to know what he was thinking. Then she decided that she didn't want to know at all because, when *twice* already she had as good as told him no, he stretched out a hand and, stroking a finger down the bridge of her nose, assured her gently, 'I'll wait.'

Josy saw that as a threat and bolted. This time Dacre let her go.

She had been in her room five minutes before the quagmire of her thoughts quietened down into a more sensible thinking pattern. Still in a daze, she ceased pacing the floor and went and sat down on the edge of her bed, all that she and Dacre had discussed still shooting through her brain.

He was tenacious, was Dacre. That whole conversation with him just now had only begun because he had been determiend to talk to her, to find out what her horrified 'No!' had been all about when he had first stated— no, bellowed—'I want you to marry me!'

She should leave; she knew that for a fact. Remembering his quiet 'I'll wait', remembering his tenacity, most definitely she should leave. And yet—she didn't want to. She didn't want to go. She loved him, was in love with him, and the thought of never seeing him again was truly, truly dreadful. So how could she leave? But how, with that threat hanging over her, could she stay?

Her head was in much the same whirl when she eventually got into her pyjamas and climbed into bed.

She had always enjoyed being alone—but she didn't want to be alone without Dacre. Her thoughts came round full circle for the umpteenth time. She wanted to stay; oh, how she wanted to stay.

In an attempt to get him off her mind she thought of everything else he had told her, and for the first time began to know a little peace of mind in one part of her life when she started to believe that it was not through her that Marc had died.

What with her having been in deep shock and French being spoken all around her, it was no wonder to her now that she had been unable to pick up on a word dropped here and there that might have resulted in her questioning and knowing that Marc had not merely fallen off Diamant through not concentrating, but had been thrown when that vicious beast had slammed him up against a tree.

Marc, poor Marc—there was so much he hadn't told her. Perhaps if she'd loved him more she would have asked more pertinent questions. Perhaps he would have told her of his wealth—even of his accident, maybe. Oh, if only he had. They'd been more well matched than he'd known. He impotent, she incapable of giving herself!

Dacre was in her head again before she went to sleep. But by morning, even though she awakened with his quietly spoken 'I'll wait' still sounding in her ears, she was calmer than she had been. Dacre could not *make* her marry him. Nobody could make her do that.

She showered and got dressed and went downstairs, thinking that perhaps Dacre would go off the idea of wanting to marry her. Perhaps he already had. But fate gave a gleeful laugh.

For just then, as she stepped down into the hall, Dacre appeared from his study and came easily towards her. 'Good morning, Josy,' he greeted her pleasantly, and to her astonishment scrutinised her face for a brief second then lowered his head and—when she thought a salute to both her cheeks might be on the way, though not strictly necessary since he had so greeted her yesterday— he instead placed a light kiss on nowhere but her mouth.

Electricity shot through her. Open-mouthed, she stared at him, but while her heart drummed and her lips still burned from the touch of his lips he did no more than place an arm about her shoulders and turn her in the direction of the breakfast-room.

'You must be as hungry as I am,' he remarked conversationally, not balking at making oblique reference to the way neither of them had finished dinner last night.

She pulled out of his arm as soon as she could without showing him how jumpy she was, but felt all over the place again. Was this the way it was going to be—the seemingly casual kiss? He had stated he wanted to marry her. Was this—a brief touching of lips, an arm light about her—his way of trying to break down her resistance?

'Ah, here's a letter for you,' he announced after he'd seen her seated and gone to his own chair. 'A female hand, I think,' he added, and, as if having satisfied himself on that account, he passed it over.

She took it from him and felt more electricity shoot through her when their hands accidentally touched. Oh, heavens, she'd be a nervous wreck if he didn't soon go back to Paris. 'Excuse me,' she murmured politely, and opened her letter.

'Not bad news?' Dacre fished for information, and, although she was as jumpy as the dickens, and all over the place emotionally, she was visited by another emotion when she discovered that she wanted to laugh at his blatant angling.

'It's from Tracey; she works at the stables,' Josy obliged, unable to hold back a smile. 'I wrote and asked her how Hetty was.'

'Hetty, your horse.' He returned her smile, his eyes on her mouth.

'Hetty, my horse,' she confirmed.

'And how is she?'

'Extremely well, apparently—but missing the titbit I usually have for her in my pocket,' she replied.

'You sound as if you're still missing her.'

'Well, she is rather special,' she defended.

And she grew all up-tight again when Dacre commented pleasantly, 'Like her owner.'

'You'll be going back to Paris today, I expect?' she said abruptly, her question coming out far more bluntly than she had meant it to.

But while she anticipated something equally blunt in reply—it was his home after all—to her surprise his reply was evenly spoken. 'I thought I might take a few weeks' holiday,' he answered.

Her glance flew to him. 'Here?' she queried worriedly, wanting with all she had nothing better, while at the same time her anxiety mounted at what she saw as more pressure.

'Here,' he confirmed, his eyes steady on hers.

'Oh,' she mumbled, and knew then that this—and he—was really, really serious.

When she went to the stables Dacre went with her. When she saddled up Nina he saddled up César. And while it was pure and utter joy to be out riding with him Josy also experienced inner conflict as she began to grow more and more worried.

Friday and Saturday followed a similar pattern—the light kiss at breakfast and Dacre's going down to the stables with her, riding with her—and Josy's nerves stretched. For, while her guilt over Marc had started to drain away and she had begun to feel as if a ton weight had lifted from her, she was still left with one very big problem—her inability to let any man get close to her.

Josy awoke on Sunday morning and her first thought was of Dacre. Oh, how she loved him. Why, oh, why had he got this idea in his head that he wanted to marry her? Why couldn't they go on as they were? Or, rather, as they had been going on.

She went down to breakfast. '*Bonjour*, Josy,' Dacre greeted her and, as he had the previous three mornings, bent his head and placed a light kiss on her mouth.

'*B-bonjour*, Dacre,' she answered, and as her nerves stretched even tauter she could not help but wonder if today would be the day she snapped—and screamed at him not to touch her.

All that day Dacre was kind and warm and gentle to her—and Josy was getting to a pitch where she wished more than ever to be back the way they had been.

'Shall we go to the *salon*?' he suggested after dinner.

'I've—er—a few things to do in my room,' she answered jerkily, and as a stern look came to his eyes, and she guessed that he was not best pleased, she said in a rush, 'Goodnight,' and left him.

Josy was up in her room when she faced the fact that she could not go on like this. For heaven's sake, she loved him and wanted to be with him. She wanted to stay in the *salon* talking with him on most any subject that came up, and for as long as he liked, but—how could she now?

And what of him? She owned that she had not given too much thought to what Dacre wanted. She supposed the reason was that she was still reeling from the fact that he had stated that he wanted to marry her—and would wait.

But she didn't want him to wait. No way did she want him to wait. He wanted a wife and, much though she loved him, that would never be her. He wanted children and, dear God, that would never, *ever* be her.

Yet was it fair that he should keep on waiting? But that was hardly her fault! She had told him no—what more could she do? Feeling bogged down by the weight of her thoughts, Josy went and took a shower. Oh, what was she going to do?

She had found no solution to the problem when, finished with her shower, she donned fresh pyjamas and got into bed. She thought she heard a door along the landing close, and realised that Dacre had left either the *salon* or his study and had called it a day.

She was still wide awake with her thoughts thirty minutes later, sleep light years away. He had to see that he was wasting his time waiting for her, didn't he? He hadn't, though, had he? In four days he hadn't. Oh, what on earth...? Surely she could do *something*?

Another half an hour went by with Josy tearing herself to shreds, not wanting to leave, by no means wanting to leave, but wondering if to do so was the only answer. Then suddenly, out of the blue, out of her utter desperation, she saw another way—and she was more awake than ever.

No way, no way! screamed her nerves. The very idea was preposterous; she just didn't have that kind of courage. Not even for him? queried a faint, wanting-to-run voice.

Oh, God, she couldn't. Just thinking about it made her tremble. Yet... She blanked her thoughts off—but they wouldn't go away. She made herself face them. She took a deep breath, and faced them.

Fact—Dacre wanted to marry her. Fact—she could not marry him. Fact—he said he would wait, but she knew he would have a lifetime's wait before she would ever marry him. And fact—she just couldn't do that to him. She had to find a way of convincing him that he was wasting his time in waiting—and there was a way. She swallowed down panic; it was that or the alternative—to leave.

But she loved him too much to leave. Did she, then, love him enough to go to him now, and let him see for himself that she could never be a wife to any man? Did she have that much courage?

Her mouth went dry at the thought—yet it wouldn't take too long. She could be back in her own bed in five minutes. She'd be distressed, of course, but she was distressed now. And did she love him or didn't she? There were at least another ten days of his holiday still to go and, from what he'd said, probably more. Was she for the next ten mornings and more to go down to breakfast in fear and trembling that his light kiss would turn to something more passionate, when she would lose control and start creating?

Unable to sit still, Josy got out of bed and began pacing up and down until, finally, she grew furious with herself and the pathetic person she felt herself to be. In the next moment she had grabbed up a robe and, shrugging into it as she went, left her room.

Her spurt of anger with herself, however, had vanished into thin air by the time she found herself outside Dacre's bedroom door. She went hot and cold all over and turned to go back to her own room, but then halted.

Just five minutes, that was all it would take! Probably less. The way things were going she was going to lose control any day now anyway—why not go in and get it over with now? She loved him, didn't she? Yes, and much too much to keep him waiting for a day that was never going to come.

A two-second burst of courage arrived. She grabbed it, taking one second to open Dacre's door and the other to step inside and close it.

The light was on; Dacre was in bed, reading. He looked up and her face went scarlet. She stayed by the door. Had she not felt rooted to the spot she would have turned and fled. But she couldn't move; every muscle and joint seemed locked.

In trauma—self-inflicted trauma—Josy watched Dacre's silent gaze on her, watched him as he closed his book.

'C...' The words wouldn't come. Dacre had his arms on top of the light coverlet; she could see his naked hair-roughened chest and just knew that he slept without pyjamas. Her insides somersaulted. She tried again. 'C-can I...?' She raised her eyes to his waiting, good-looking face. That thought, 'waiting', spurred her on. 'Can I sl-sleep with you?' she asked on one gasp of breath.

Silently, unspeaking, Dacre studied her panicking expression. But just as her every instinct started to clamour out that she should not have come, 'Of course,' he answered obligingly.

For several seconds her feet refused to obey her brain's instruction to go forward. But, after an agony of wanting to turn tail, Josy moved and approached the double bed.

Once more obligingly, Dacre moved over to allow her a half-share. She swallowed, but when her hands went to the tie of her robe she found that, for all that she was pyjama-clad underneath, she just could not take her robe off with him watching.

And she loved him more than ever when, for all the world as if he understood, he murmured, 'It's all right, *petite*,' and, turning from her, he placed his book down on his bedside table and put out the light.

By that time, though, she was shaking so much that she could barely get the hurriedly tied-up knot undone. Eventually she managed it, but only by telling herself that she was doing this for him was she able to remove her robe and find her way under the light coverlet.

Despite it being from her great love for him, though, it was still tensely, while keeping as much distance from him as possible, that she lay there, ramrod-stiff.

She felt him move, and was shaking so much by then that she knew he could feel it too. He came closer and, propping himself on one elbow, as if by some automatic radar, he placed an arm about her waist. 'Hush, little Josy, I won't harm you,' he promised softly. But she was beyond answering.

She could feel his arm, warm about her rigid, shaking body, and she loved him so much—and she wanted to cry at the thought that soon, out of her control, she would be fighting him from her.

Every one of her senses seemed heightened; she even felt the warmth of his breath as his face came nearer. She could feel his chest against her, and as panic tried to get a deeper grip—she froze. She clenched her hands tightly, her nails digging into her palms, when gently Dacre placed his lips over hers and kissed her oh, so tenderly, neither demanding nor taking, but a longer kiss than those of breakfast-time.

Then his mouth left hers, and he took his arm from across her, and Josy waited for the dreadful onslaught that was to come as he gently stroked the side of her face.

But the onslaught never came. For, even while Josy knew that at any moment now all hell was going to break loose in her as she fought a battle with fear and lost, to her absolute astonishment Dacre kissed her briefly just once more, and then breathed, 'Goodnight, little one,' and turned over—and went to sleep!

CHAPTER SEVEN

DAWN was breaking when Josy awoke, and for all of one second she didn't know where she was. Then she became aware of another human form lying beside her, and in a bound of movement, her heart pounding, she was out of that bed.

Snatching up her robe *en route*—no time to put it on— she went for the door. She did not stop running until she was safely in her own room, and everything that had happened—which she had to admit was very little— played back in her mind.

With the coming of daylight it seemed absolutely incredible that she, shy Josy Fereday, had from somewhere found the temerity to go and get into bed with a man!

Oh, not just any man—agreed. And she had asked his permission first. But, great heavens, had that been her? With the coming of day she could only gasp at her nerve.

Without a doubt there *was* something magical about this place. Three months ago she could never have seen herself acting as she had last night. Even a month ago she would have scorned the very idea—but a month ago, while now she faced the fact she had been learning to love Dacre, she hadn't known that she was in love with him, and being in love had made all the difference.

She sat in a bedroom chair, her knees to her chin, her arms around her shins. Love made all the difference... Her eyes grew dreamy as she remembered the wonderful tenderness of Dacre's kiss last night.

Strange that she hadn't been alarmed by it. Fearful, yes—next door to terrified wasn't perhaps overstating it—but that wonderful tender kiss had not alarmed her.

When the time came for her to go down to breakfast Josy was again wondering at her nerve. Grief, he had been naked! And she had not only lain in bed with him but—admittedly after hours of lying wide awake—she had gradually stopped shaking and had even fallen asleep for a few hours.

She left her room, not knowing how she was going to face him again after what she'd done, and with a cowardly part of her half wishing that he had decided to return to Paris and had already left.

But he had not gone to Paris, and, as if he had known the precise second she would leave her room, was there in the hall just as she stepped down into it.

She knew the futility of wishing that she would not go scarlet when she next saw him and went crimson when he greeted her softly, 'Hello, *ma brave*.' His eyes raked her flushed skin and, having called her courageous, he bent and kissed her.

'Er—g-good morning.' She struggled to find her voice.

Dacre smiled. 'Breakfast,' he decreed briskly—and so the day began.

And it was a good day—a day that seemed to Josy to be better than previous days even though they did much the same thing. Together they attended the horses, and together they exercised them, sometimes in silence and sometimes talking. Dacre seemed prepared to answer the smallest and the largest questions she asked, while in between he asked his own questions of her—even drawing from her the reluctant admission that she played the piano quite well.

'Why did I tell you that?' she questioned in amazement as they returned to the house around four that afternoon after a long walk across fields and through woods.

'You didn't—I dragged it from you, Mademoiselle Modeste,' he grinned.

'Oh, well, that's all right, then,' she laughed and, laughter in her heart, and in her eyes too, she thought she had better make herself scarce before Dacre saw a hint of how she felt about him.

He had mentioned having to check something out in his study, and at the stairs she went to part from him. 'Shall we have dinner out tonight, *petite*?' His question stopped her.

She looked at him, her lovely brown eyes larger than ever. She opened her mouth, but couldn't think of one good reason why she shouldn't go out with him. 'Agathe will have already begun some sort of preparation for...' some self-preservation instinct found a small objection anyway.

He shook his head. 'She knew this morning that my...' he paused, and she waited for the word 'cousin'. 'My *amie* and I might dine out this evening.'

'Oh,' Josy mumbled. 'Yes, then.' And, remembering her manners, she added politely, 'I'd like to,' and went quickly up to her room.

The day had been super, but she was starting to get agitated again. When had she stopped being his cousin to become his *amie*—his friend? And that 'Shall we have dinner out tonight?'—not 'Would you like to', or 'May I take you', but more comfortable than that as if—as if he thought of them as an item and wanted her to think that way—'Shall we', as though whatever they would be doing it would be together.

Josy tried to put her worries behind her as she got ready that evening, but it wasn't easy. He was waiting, she reminded herself. Beneath it all, beneath the friendly conversation, the companionship of riding together, of walking side by side, of being her friend, he was still quietly waiting.

'You wore that dress on your first evening here,' Dacre commented, when, wearing her dress of deep apricot, she went into the *salon*. It surprised her that he remembered, but he was such a charming friend to be with that night that the evening flew by—and she started to wish that it might never end.

'I shall have to stop eating like this.' She laughed at the frothy, creamy confection Dacre had ordered for her as their meal came to an end.

'I can't see that you've put on weight,' he returned. 'But you are looking much better than when you first came to me.'

She knew that he was right. Given that she had a pale complexion that never seemed to tan, she had a tinge more colour and, with Dacre having told her all he had of Marc's two accidents, her guilt seemed a thing of the past.

But Dacre's 'when you first came to me' began to get to her. When they returned home she left him securing the house with a jerky kind of, 'Thank you for the evening; goodnight,' and went to her room, reading the word 'waiting' in that possessive-sounding part of the phrase 'to me'.

By the time she had taken a shower and donned her pyjamas she found herself on the same emotion-tearing treadmill that she had been on last night. Only tonight, having spent a most wonderful day with Dacre, a new dimension had been added. She now knew that with all her heart and soul she wanted to marry him! Just as she knew with every scrap of logic she had that that could never be.

How could it? The moment he touched her, not as a friend but as a lover, she would go to pieces. She knew it as if it had been seared into her brain. And he was 'waiting'!

Josy had been sleepless in her bed for two hours with the agony she had gone through last night seeming intensified that night—perhaps because of the wonderful day she had spent with him.

Anger—with herself, with him, with her sleeplessness—she was tired, felt worn out, yet still couldn't go to sleep—was the prod she needed to get crossly out of her bed to go and do something about it. To go and get it over with once and for all!

This time, however, she went so fast that she didn't even wait to put on her robe, which made it just as well that when speedily, if quietly, she entered Dacre's bedroom she found his room in darkness.

She halted just where she was, knowing he was asleep and that she shouldn't have come. Her anger gone, she went to back silently from his room, and then discovered that Dacre wasn't asleep after all, and that he knew she was there. 'Come to bed, little one,' he instructed her in the darkness, his voice all soothing and calm.

Her throat went dry again, and for long, long seconds she couldn't move. Then, barely aware what she was doing, like someone in a trance, she quietly closed the door and went over to the bed.

Her nerves started to plague her with a vengeance when she slipped in between the covers. Without touching him, she could feel his warmth. But he had his back to her, and made no move to turn to her, and all of a sudden she was overwhelmed by the enormity of what she had done. Dacre didn't want her in his bed! To come in the way she had, to get into bed with him was an imposition!

Mortified, she went to scramble out but somehow got tangled up with the bedding—and then suddenly she became aware that the piece of material she held in her hand was not bedding, nor was it her pyjamas—it was the jacket of *his* pyjamas!

Oh, Dacre, I love you. She stopped trying to get out of his bed. He had been expecting her—must have wanted her in his bed—or why, when he was a sleep-in-the-nude type of man, was he suffering to wear pyjamas?

She lay back down, her shaking settling down to a more healthy tremble. Dacre still had his back to her, but he stretched backwards with his left arm to touch her.

'Try to get some sleep,' he suggested kindly, and while she quiveringly took from that that he was more interested in sleeping himself than in attempting to make love to her he took his arm away.

Josy lay for some while trying to figure him out. The virile look of him, the very fact of his sophistication, plus the added fact that he had so easily asked her if she and Marc had made love before they married ruled out the idea the he held any pious 'no sex before marriage' views. So why? Was it her? Did she put him off?

How could she put him off, though? He had spoken of marriage, of children... Mists of sleep snatched at her. She moved, turned over on to her side—and then discovered that she had turned over to face Dacre's sleeping back.

Oh, how she loved him. She stretched out a hand to touch him; somehow she seemed unable to resist it. He didn't move. She edged a little nearer, finding comfort, warmth in his nearness. Still he didn't move. She edged nearer still, until there was just an inch or so separating them. And she wanted to touch him, to hold him. Hardly daring to breathe, she placed a tentative arm around his waist. His hand was there; she touched it.

'Goodnight, Josy,' he said lightly, and, taking her hand in his, he gave it a light squeeze.

She gave a start, and for about three seconds held her breath. Then she mumbled chokily, 'Goodnight, Dacre,' and a few minutes later began to feel really drowsy. Without thinking, she took her head from her pillow and laid her cheek against the warmth of his pyjama-clad back. She hadn't known that sleeping with the one you love could be so wonderful.

She awoke to find that it was morning—and could not remember when she had slept so well. She had no idea of the time, but from the strength of daylight realised that she had slept way past her usual waking time.

She had the bed to herself and guessed that Dacre must have been up and about for an age. Her brain suggested that she should hurry back to her room, but she found she liked being in Dacre's bed. She touched the place where he had lain, and loved him so much that it was like a physical ache.

Then the sound of the door of the adjoining bathroom opening caused her mind to go a total blank. And when Dacre, freshly showered, a towel around his middle his only covering, stepped into the bedroom she didn't know where to look.

'I—er—slept late,' she choked, and was half out of bed, ready to dive for the door, before she became aware of her own thin covering.

'So did I,' Dacre answered conspiratorially, and at the smile in his voice she looked across to him. She looked to his eyes; there was a watchful kind of smile in them, and on his mouth. 'You looked so beautiful lying there that it seemed a sin to disturb you,' he added conversationally.

She didn't know how she felt at the intimation that he had been looking at her while she had been asleep. 'Yes, well,' she said, which meant nothing, but which she hoped passed for an answer as she measured the distance from the bed to the door. 'I'd—er—better go and...' As the words left her she moved from the bed.

She had only gone a few steps, though, when he enquired, 'No morning kiss for me?' and she halted, mid-flight.

She turned. Dacre had greeted her every morning with a kiss. And albeit that that kiss had always taken place downstairs, with both of them fully dressed, it seemed— after having invited herself to his bed—a little churlish to be—um—stuffy about it.

Josy moved a little towards him and was glad that he came and met her halfway. She looked at him and still wanted to run—but found to her surprise that, thinly pyjama-clad as she was, she wanted to stay.

'Good morning,' she greeted him, and when he made no move to kiss her she stared silently at him, her expression serious.

Still he did not move. There was about a foot separating them. His naked chest was so close that she could have touched it. Nervously she stepped closer—and then reached up and touched her lips fleetingly to his.

Josy pulled back and stared at him. He said nothing, neither threatening nor looking ready to embrace her. And all at once, while she stood there warily watching him and her heart started to pound, she knew that she wanted to kiss him again.

She looked at him silently waiting. Did he want her to kiss him again? He wasn't walking away, was he? Josy moved a few inches closer, her body almost touching his, and shyly, nervously, but mainly because she didn't seem able to stop herself, she again stretched up and placed her lips against his—this time for a little longer. And that was when, just as she was going to break away from him and hurry back to her room, Dacre moved.

Josy felt his arms come about her. But although she jerked back instinctively she didn't fight to break out of his loose hold. Feeling slightly amazed that though her heart was beating nineteen to the dozen she was still there, Josy stared at him all large-eyed and, she had to own to herself, apprehensive.

'Don't worry,' he breathed softly. 'It will be all right.'

Would it? She didn't think so! On past performance, when she thought of the terrified way she had fought against Marc's physical aggression, she was sure it wouldn't be so. Which was why she was further amazed to hear herself ask, albeit a touch shakily, 'C-can I—kiss you again?'

Dacre smiled. 'I'd like that,' he answered.

Solemnly Josy eyed him. She felt she wanted to kiss him—but she wasn't certain. Nor was she certain about anything else for a few seconds, because, without haste, Dacre was helping her out and, not waiting for her to kiss him, was all at once claiming her lips—in the first lingering kiss they had shared.

Her knees went so weak that she placed her hands on his waist to hold herself steady. She felt his firm male body—and let go of him as though burned. But she had no need to worry about falling over for Dacre's arms about her tightened, and suddenly, while realising that she had never felt so secure or at the same time so bewildered, Josy moved to pull out of his hold.

'Are you all right?' he asked, releasing her immediately, his eyes searching hers.

'I'm—not sure,' she replied honestly.

And Dacre, after a moment more of looking into her eyes, unexpectedly smiled, and teased, 'Then I suggest, sweet Josy, that you meet me downstairs for breakfast.'

'Oh, Dacre.' She laughed, and, feeling all light-headed suddenly, quickly went back to her own room.

Another wonderful day followed. They walked together, talked together, and, when they were taking their ease by a stream, Dacre picked a wild flower and tucked it behind her ear. Even as her skin tingled from his touch she loved him for the gesture.

They had dinner at their usual time, but as the meal drew to an end so she started to feel tense. A closeness seemed to have sprung up from nowhere between her and Dacre, and she was starting to realise that she liked that closeness. But still at the back of her mind was the knowledge that nothing was ever going to come of it.

'Do you want to share it with me?' Dacre's voice in the silence of her thoughts startled her, causing her to realise that he had noticed her change of mood.

She shook her head. 'No,' she replied, and, aware by now that he was unlikely to let her leave it there, added, 'I'm—er—feeling a bit—uptight.'

For long moments he eyed her steadily and, making her feel terribly guilty, looked just as if he thought her being uptight was all his fault. 'I'm sorry,' he apologised. 'I didn't want that.'

'Oh, Dacre,' she said quickly, and was so confused all at once. 'I think I need to be on my own—do you mind if I don't come into the *salon*?'

She looked into his eyes, but could tell nothing of what he was thinking. 'Of course not,' he said, and Josy left him—and knew that she would not be going along to his bedroom that night.

In fact, a few hours later, when she lay sleepless in her bed, she was beginning to wonder how she had ever found the nerve to do what she had. And yet, she then realised, she had truly liked sleeping with him.

Over the last few days she felt that she had got to know him better than any man she knew. Talking to him by day, sharing his bed by night—it was an intimacy she enjoyed. But truly it couldn't go on like this.

A few more hours passed, with Josy loving Dacre and knowing that he should never learn of it. She grew more tense than ever, wanting to go to him while knowing that never again would she go and get into his bed. Her nerve supply had run out, leaving her wanting to go to him, and anxious, and emotionally all over the place.

And then, just as she was about to hit rock bottom, her bedroom door opened and closed. And into the darkness, for all the world as if he knew she would be awake, Dacre said softly, 'I couldn't sleep without you.'

A mixture of joy to have him near mingled with a familiar apprehension. 'We—um—can't have that,' she answered, and moved over to make room for him.

'Are you still feeling tense, *chérie*?' he enquired as he joined her beneath the light coverlet.

'It's—nothing,' she answered.

'Sit up.'

'S-sit up?' she queried.

'I'll massage the back of your neck,' he offered matter-of-factly.

'It won't do any good.' She had no intention of sitting up.

'How do you know?'

'Oh—you!' she exclaimed, and loved him—and, perhaps a little nervously, she laughed.

But sit up she did. She presented him with her back—and braced herself for his touch. And, when it came, like everything else there it seemed to be magical.

He applied firm but gentle pressure, and she wanted to lean against him. 'Undo your top,' he ordered lightly, and she was all quivering tension again.

'Why?'

'Because I can't get at you properly—and you've knots of tension all the way down your spine.'

He was probably right there. She felt tense all the way down to her toes. And, after several minutes of thinking she'd be hanged if she would undo her pyjama jacket, she found her fingers going to the fastening.

She knew that he was aware her jacket was undone when, with a small tug at the material, he had the freedom he needed to work with. She felt his hands, warm on the skin of her back, and thought she might faint from the shock of it.

'You've—er...' Her husky voice faded altogether; he'd got the most wonderful hands. 'You've—um—done this before?' she asked, after a moment or two of getting her breath back.

'You're my first patient,' Dacre replied, gently moulding her spine, his voice—so close.

'H-how do you know what to do, then?'

'I was once a weekend guest at the house of some friends. The only book they'd got that I hadn't read was one on this subject.' He paused, and added matter-of-factly, 'I'm glad I bothered to open it.'

Josy couldn't have answered him then if she had wanted to, because although his voice might have sounded matter-of-fact his hands were telling her something different. For, while he was still massaging her gently, those movements at her back seemed to her to be more caressing than massaging. She could be wrong, of course, but... 'I'm all right now,' she said on a choky kind of sharp sound.

His hands stilled. 'You want me to stop?' he breathed, and when she didn't answer he moved her long fair hair to one side and placed a gentle kiss on the side of her neck. She tensed. 'You're beautiful.' he murmured. 'Your skin is like silk.' She swallowed. 'And I'd like to feel more of it,' he stated gently.

'W-would you?' This wasn't right. She knew it wasn't right—so why wasn't she screaming? Why was she sitting there? Why wasn't she yelling?

'Let me take this from you,' he suggested, his fingers on her pyjama top.

'Wh-why?'

'Oh, *petite*!' There was a smile in his voice. But, if he thought she should know why without him having to tell her, he refrained from uttering it but said softly instead, 'Little darling, it's time to let go some of your modesty.'

'Is it?' she asked croakily—and had her answer in the way that gently, unhurriedly he removed her pyjama jacket from her.

She pulled her arms forward to cover her naked breasts, and swallowed hard as he traced the tenderest of kisses over her shoulders. Then, while she was still coming to terms with that tenderness, those kisses, that all over tingling inside her, Dacre's hands came around her waist. He gathered her closer, and as her back came into contact with his hair-sprinkled chest so she realised with a start of alarm, that he was not wearing a pyjama top either!

'Shh—don't be alarmed,' he gentled her when she moved, startled—and for long moments he held her like that, still, close to him, as if to allow her to get used to the feel of him.

Josy had never experienced such intimacy. But after a minute or so her jumpy nerves began to settle. Oh,

Dacre—she wanted to call his name, to tell him that what he wanted would never be.

She leaned back against him, a sadness in her heart. She did not doubt that this was as intimate as she would ever get with any man. Or was it? Suddenly, as his hands about her waist pulled her more against him, so those hands began tenderly to caress over her stomach. She swallowed as with whispering traces Dacre caressed upwards nearer her breasts.

'Keep breathing—I'll let nothing harm you,' he murmured in her ear, aware of her sucked-in and held breath. Gradually his hands found their way beneath her shielding arms, caressing beneath the guard they kept over her breasts, and then, as she stopped breathing altogether, his right hand moved up to her right breast, until—after an agony of suspense—he eventually held her breast captive in his palm.

'Dacre!' she cried.

'It's all right. It's all right,' he soothed, and, turning her, he released her breast and held her safe in his arms, quiet, up against his heart. 'Shh, sweet flower,' he soothed. 'You'll be fine.'

What she was, Josy realised, was totally bewildered. She had thought herself bewildered before, but that had been before Dacre had held her breast and her discovery—that she liked it!

Gently then he kissed her. And Josy wasn't sure about anything any more. 'If you want me to go you've only to say,' he breathed, his cheek against her cheek, 'but I'd very much like to stay.'

'To—sl-sleep?' she asked.

He paused before answering. Then, 'To sleep, little love,' he confirmed.

'Please stay,' she invited, and together they lay down.

And Josy liked that too. Dacre kept an arm about her and she rested her head on his shoulder. Whatever happened, she would always have these moments to remember.

'Goodnight,' she said.

'Goodnight, *petite*,' he answered, and placed a light kiss on her brow.

And that was when Josy discovered that she wasn't sleepy, and that, since it was unlikely that she would sleep with Dacre again, she wanted to know the feel of his skin. She took her hand from across his waist and raised it to stroke across his chest. She loved the warmth of him. She guessed he was asleep, and with feather-light movements so as not to wake him, she investigated his shoulders, his chest, her curious fingers exploring his manly nipples.

She found the hair on his chest intriguing, and had just obeyed an impulse to follow a line of hair down to where his navel met the waistband of his pyjama bottoms when Dacre's deep—and disturbed—voice sounded in the darkness. 'Sweet flower, I'm only human.'

Startled, she realised that he had been awake to every one of her exploring movements. 'G-goodnight!' she said jerkily, and hurriedly took her hand back to where it had been before.

Dacre was gone when she awakened in the morning. But she remembered with sweetness, not fear the way he had caressed her in the small hours, the way she had explored him. He had cradled her to sleep and it had been beautiful.

He was there to greet her when she went down to breakfast. 'No problems?' he asked when he took her, blushing, into the loose circle of his arms. She shook her head, realising that he was asking if she was this morning resenting his intimate caresses. '*Bon*!' he murmured, and, with a light kiss to her mouth that lingered perhaps a second longer than it should have, he started her day.

And it was another wonderful day. They rode together in the morning and walked together in the afternoon, and as Josy got ready to go down to dinner that night she realised that, their discussions having been many and varied, they had talked over far more matters than she had ever done with Marc.

With Marc it had been horses and horses to the exclusion of everything else. And while she had been quite content with that at the time—given that by mutual consent a non-physical relationship had been agreed upon—would a daily diet of nothing but horse talk have been enough to sustain her?

She felt guilty thinking such thoughts, but it was a fact that she felt far more mentally stimulated after her discussions with Dacre than she had ever done with Marc. Oh, she would always love horses, she knew that. Her love of animals—horses in particular—must be something she had been born with. Just thinking of Hetty made her want to see her. But...

Josy left her room, suddenly aware that since knowing Dacre, and not least since falling in love with him, she had become more mentally—and physically, if she was honest—alive.

She was having dinner with him a short while later when he looked across the table to her and excused himself from joining her in the *salon* later. 'I've a little business to attend to this evening—it could take a while.'

'Oh,' she murmured, and was about to add that she would have an early night when several things struck her at once. Did he mean that he intended to work in his study, or was he going out? And, if he *was* going out, wasn't it a funny time to be going out to do business?

Realising that she was in the throes of nothing more than jealousy, Josy forced herself to recognise that in the business world work did not cease on the stroke of five.

Hot on the heels of that thought came another far more unpalatable thought. Oh, dear heaven, Dacre would be going back to Paris soon to look after his business. She had just spent a week of being almost exclusively in his company—how on earth was she going to cope, not seeing him every day?

'You look a little downcast, *ma chère*. Is something troubling you?'

She shook her head and saw that he was silently watching. And if she had learned anything about him, about herself, in the week she had just spent with him it was that, somehow or other, she always ended up answering his questions. And, since she seemed totally unable to lie, she began, 'Well, to be honest—' and broke off.

'Your honesty is something else I admire about you,' he inserted—which threw her completely. He admired her! Well, something about her anyway. 'Why so sad?' he asked insistently.

'Well, not sad exactly; I was just—er—thinking that—er—this has been a very pleasant holiday...' oh, grief, it was his holiday not hers '...and that—er—I think I'm—er—I'm going to—um—miss you a little next week.'

Dacre stilled and just looked at her. Then very quietly he remarked, 'I think, *ma petite*, that that is the nicest thing you've ever said to me.'

While Josy went a little pink, and with his look still steady on her, he paused for some seconds. Then, as if encouraged by what she had just said, he proceeded to cause her to stare back at him speechlessly, her heart thundering, when he asked deliberately, 'Perhaps, my dear, you would invite me to stay with you tonight?'

She stared, knowing that he meant in her bed. And her first reaction was to say a very positive, No, no, no. Because from that steady, determined look in his eyes, and the way he had said it, she just knew that if she said, as she had last night, 'To sleep?' that he would tell her, No.

She opened her mouth to say, I can't, but with his grey eyes holding her steady the words just wouldn't come. Somehow he seemed to be willing her to say yes.

Her throat felt dry. 'I'm—scared,' she confessed huskily—and still his eyes held hers steady.

'I know,' he acknowledged calmly—but didn't seem ready to let go.

'Wh-what if I panic?' If? There was no question in her mind. 'Oh, I ca—'

'You won't,' he told her evenly.

'Yes, but what if I do? You'll—'

'We'll handle it,' Dacre soothed, and, with the smile she needed to see breaking, said, 'Stop worrying about it, little flower—just give me the yes I'm waiting to hear.'

She took a deep breath. 'Y-yes.' She gulped and, albeit nervously, gave him a weak smile.

'Josy,' he said softly, and just at that moment Agathe came in to tell him he was wanted on the telephone. 'Excuse me, my dear,' he requested, getting to his feet. 'It's a call I've been waiting for.' With that he left the dining-room.

There was a phone in the hall, but when Josy could hear no sound of his voice she guessed that he was taking the call in his study. It seemed a good time to return to her room.

First one hour dragged by and then another. She had to start with paced her room, and then showered, got into fresh pyjamas, and paced some more. Half of her wished that he would soon come, so she could get this over with. The other half of her wanted to call it off altogether. What if she panicked as she had with Marc?

Oh, God! She began pacing again, knowing that it wasn't a matter of not seeing Dacre next week when he went back to Paris. Suddenly she knew that if she lost control and it all went wrong then tomorrow she would have to leave for England. She had been fooling herself in thinking that she could stay.

She calmed down a little when she recalled the sweetness of the way he had gently cupped her breast last night. She hadn't panicked then, had she? Perhaps it would be all right. Even if she couldn't believe that it would be, perhaps it might. She clung on to that thought; the alternative—to leave—was too awful.

Yet she was saddened when she went and got into bed because by then she had accepted that leaving was her only choice.

All this—her going along to Dacre's room—had only started because she had wanted him to witness for himself that he was wasting his time waiting in the belief that she might marry him and be the mother of his children. She had, she must own, rather lost sight of that. But now, for his sake, it had to end. She loved him enough to do that. The worst part of it, though, was that whereas before she had hoped she might be able to stay she now knew that after tonight she would have to go.

It was around midnight when Dacre entered her room. He was tall, broad-shouldered, wearing a bathrobe and, on seeing his bare legs beneath, Josy knew he had on nothing else.

He stood there, his hand on the light switch. 'Forgive me for being so long. My business took longer than I'd anticipated,' he apologised.

'You must be tired,' she replied without thinking, and wanted to groan out loud at the realisation that he might think that that was some last minute suggestion that he should go straight to sleep. He did not answer but switched off the light and plunged the room into darkness.

Josy started to shake the moment he got into bed with her. 'Hey, I thought we had done away with all that?' he teased, and she loved him, and loved his teasing, and had no objection to make when he reached for her.

The arm he placed about her was uncovered, his naked chest near her hand. 'I n-need a light on,' she gasped.

'*Certainement.*' There was warmth in his voice, and she loved him some more that he wasn't cross with her, but at once took his arm from around her and, leaning to his side of the bed, switched on the bedside lamp. Then he adjusted the shade so that the room was shadowed—a mere subdued and subtle lighting—and turned back to her. He did not place an arm around her but, propping himself up, looked down at her.

'I'm sorry,' she apologised.

'Oh, sweet Josy,' he smiled. 'You're scared and worried, I know. But I'm no different from the man you've slept with these last three nights.'

'I know.' She tried to smile back but couldn't. 'But— it's d-different tonight, isn't it?'

He looked at her, and then moved further into bed with her. She could smell the recently showered smell of him as he leaned to her and gently kissed the side of her face. 'Only if you want it to be,' he assured her, and, placing a kiss to the corner of her mouth, added, 'Believe me, my dear, whatever happens, should you feel panic or fear, there is no way that I'll force myself on you.'

'Oh, Dacre!' she cried, and took one arm out of the bed so that she could touch his face. She knew then that he was telling her that there wasn't even the smallest likelihood that he would lose control and start tearing at her clothes as Marc had.

'Trust me,' he urged, and, taking hold of her hand, he placed a kiss in her palm.

Josy closed her eyes, and a moment later felt the warmth of him as he moved nearer. She opened her eyes and saw his dear face near, and she smiled, and when lightly he placed his lips over hers she took her other hand from beneath the coverlet and put her arms round him.

His back was warm, hard-muscled and all male. And, just as her hands had explored his chest last night, she stroked them softly over his back. Dacre broke his tender kiss to look at her. Then, seeming to enjoy her lips, he kissed her again, more lingeringly this time.

I'm not panicking, she thought, and stared solemnly at him when he raised his head again. 'You've—um—' She broke off to cough, her voice all choky and almost inaudible. 'You've got a nice back,' she told him huskily, and he kissed first one eye and then the other.

'And so, Josy, have you,' he answered, one hand somehow finding its way under the top of her pyjamas. She felt the warmth of his hand on her midriff and tensed. 'Relax, sweet flower, relax,' he murmured, and placed his lips over hers and gently kept them there while sensitive fingers stroked and caressed beneath her thin covering.

Subtly then, for with all her heightened senses she was aware the whole time, the tenor of his kisses gradually began to change. His kiss became firmer, longer, his hold that bit stronger.

His hands ceased their caressing movements on her skin, and the next she knew was that she felt one hand at the buttons of her pyjama jacket. He did not immediately unbutton it, though, but, as if asking her permission, first kissed her and then looked at her.

'As you said—it's—um—time I let go of some of my m-modesty,' she managed chokily.

'My brave Josy,' Dacre murmured, and undid one button and bent to kiss that place, and Josy gripped on to him but did not panic.

Nor did she panic when he undid the next button and parted the material and kissed the skin beneath. When the last button was undone he gently raised her, holding her to him while he took her pyjama top from her. Tender words in French left him then as he held her, her breasts naked against him.

And Josy clutched on to him. She felt shy; she felt nervous but, she realised, she trusted him, and something in her started to relax. She felt his hands caressing at her back. 'Oh, Dacre,' she murmured, loving him so.

'Don't be afraid, little one. I have you safe,' he breathed, and she wanted to kiss him—and had to tell him so.

'I want to kiss you.' She gulped—and could not believe the long, drawn-out shaky sigh that left him.

'I so hoped you would,' he invited, and, holding her to him, he lay down, drawing her half over him. 'Kiss me, sweet life,' he added.

She stared down into his eyes. 'I'm not very good at it,' she confessed.

'You will be,' he assured her confidently, and she gave a little laugh; incredibly, she wasn't shaking any more!

She lowered her head and placed her mouth over his. She felt his hands come to move her more over him, and swallowed when she felt the caress of his touch as he captured her breasts, found the hardened peaks, and moulded them to cause such delight in her that she wanted more.

'Dacre!' she gasped.

'You're all right—it's natural,' he assured her, just as if he knew all about the excitement that was starting to build up in her.

'Is it?'

'Oh, yes.' He smiled, and she loved him and lowered her head to explore his mouth once more.

She pulled back; he had a wonderful mouth. She felt hypnotised by it, and bent to him, kissing him, looking at him again, and, hardly knowing what she was doing, but somehow as if wanting to taste him, she touched his mouth with the tip of her tongue.

An exclamation in French escaped him and a spasm of movement took him. 'Did I do something wrong?' she asked.

'Sweet Josy, carry on like that and you'll soon be graduating with honours.'

'Oh,' she said, and buried her face in his neck—and liked what he was doing to her when he rolled her over and took over the kissing tuition.

She felt his hands warm on her back, warm on her breasts, but, having thought that she had broken through those high barriers of modesty, found that she was over-whelmed by shyness again when he pulled back his head so that he could see her nudity.

She tried to cover herself, and heard him laugh softly. 'You are a true delight,' he murmured, and lowered his head, and as her hands fell away he kissed first one breast and then the other—and a fire of wanting started to lick into life within her. She gave a gasp, and immediately Dacre raised his head. 'Josy?'

'I...' she managed—and had to tell him. 'I think—I want to... I think I want you!'

His glance stayed with her; she saw a smile break on him, and, every bit as if he understood her bewilderment, gently it was that he asked, 'Would you like to find out for sure?'

She knew what he was asking, and for the first time panicked a little. 'Help me,' she pleaded.

'Oh, my darling,' he crooned, and gathered her in his arms and held her quietly for long moments, and then gradually, and still quietly, he began to stroke and caress her to a higher peak of wanting.

Josy felt his hands, his fingertips, at her breasts, stroking them and peaking them to hardened points of perfection. She kissed him, and he kissed her. She kissed his nipples, and he moulded the exquisite pink tips of her breasts with his tongue and mouth.

She felt his hands at the waistband of her pyjama trousers. 'Dacre,' she whispered.

'I know, sweet darling—it'll be all right,' he soothed, and unhurriedly he undid the fastening, and as unhurriedly took her only covering from her.

She wanted her pyjamas back—but didn't want them. It was a warm night and the light bedcover had disappeared to the floor by that time. Shyness took Josy again when he lowered his head to kiss her belly and thighs. 'Dacre!' she cried in alarm, and he was back with her.

'Shh, sweet love, you're doing fine,' he encouraged, and gently kissed her. But as his kiss deepened so more fire shot through her and her body, and with no thought of inhibitions she wanted to get closer to him.

She pressed near to him, and felt shock ripple through her when she came up against the waiting masculine wanting of him. She backed away, clutching fiercely at him as she fought through another barricade of shyness and panic.

And Dacre was marvellous. For, just as though he understood that this was another giant hurdle for her, he whispered encouraging words to her, kissing her, gentling her, moulding her silken body, his sensitive fingers a whispering caress.

And as her inhibitions started to fade and it was all so wonderful she wanted to tell him that she loved him. But she knew she could not. So she kissed him, and as he caressed her so that fire that had never died started to burn more fiercely than ever.

She lightly touched his body, loved his firm hips. 'Stay calm, my love,' he breathed softly, and whispered his touch to her thighs—and she stayed calm while he came closer and she again felt his wonderful body next to hers. He moved against her and she could only wonder at this freedom—this wonderful, wonderful freedom—as with kisses and caresses he took her to yet new heights.

Their legs intertwined as his magical, sensitive fingers made her body sing, and she sighed in pleasure and in love; he kissed her. Soon, she knew, he would make her his, and as her whole body throbbed out her need for him she was no longer afraid.

CHAPTER EIGHT

DACRE had gone when Josy awakened in the morning. The sun shone brilliantly through her bedroom window and she opened her eyes to a feeling of contentment and joy. She moved over to the spot where Dacre had lain and put her head on his pillow.

She remembered his wonderful lovemaking, his tenderness, and loved him with the whole of her being. How caring of her he had been, how patient. Oh, that magical togetherness. And, joy of all joys, she wasn't frigid as she had supposed. Not with him—her love.

Josy closed her eyes as she recalled the exquisite pleasure of his sensitive lovemaking. She had tried not to cry out at the initial pain of sharing her untried body with him but had been unable to prevent herself from sucking in her breath.

'Oh, forgive me, my dear one,' Dacre had whispered, kissing her and caressing her and waiting until the spasm had passed. And only when he'd judged that she was over that moment had he caringly made her his.

Josy opened her eyes on that word 'caringly'. Did he care? Her heart started to hammer; he had said he wanted to marry her, hadn't he? Suddenly a riot of thoughts and questions began to bombard her, making it impossible for her to stay in her bed.

She headed for the shower, but those thoughts and questions followed her. Did he care for her? That question pounded again and again in her head.

She had found no answer, when, showered and dressed, she discovered that she was reluctant to go and

seek him out. In a way, she supposed, without compre-
hending how it was possible after having lain naked with
him through the night, there were still pockets of shyness
in her.

She guessed that she might always be shy to some
degree. You couldn't change overnight. But—and here
her breath caught—what she had discovered overnight
was that she could be—a wife! Her mouth dried at the
thought. Dacre, with time, patience and understanding,
had shown her that. The problem, admittedly aided by
her inexperience and reserve, had been Marc's!

But she didn't want to think of Marc—poor, dear
Marc—just then. Just then it was quite momentous
enough to take on board the discovery of her own normality and—her heartbeats quickened—the fact that she
could marry Dacre—if he still wanted to marry her!

She brushed her hair at the dressing-table but, brush
in hand, a shadow came to her joy in that morning.
Perhaps Dacre wouldn't want to marry her—not now;
not now that he had lain with her. He wasn't like that,
though; she ousted the doubt. Besides, she trusted him.
And no man could be the tender, considerate way he had
been with her last night and... But what did she know
of men? Why had Dacre wanted to marry her? Perhaps
he didn't any more?

A mental pain started to nip that was almost physical.
But her mental anguish halted abruptly, all thoughts
fleeing, when just then the handle of her bedroom door
turned. Josy stared, hypnotised, unaware that she was
on her feet. Then as the door opened and, not pausing
to knock, Dacre came in she felt her face go scarlet.

He looked at her. Silently, his expression serious, as
if he was weighing up her reaction, he studied her, and
as shyness threatened to choke her she sought for some-

thing to say that would get her through this un-comfortable moment.

'Good morning,' she managed, and hastily looked at the carpet, wanting to die. Grief—not too many hours ago she had been manifestly less formal!

She was not left to suffer miserably for long, however. For, while she was still finding the carpet of utmost interest, a pair of expensive male shoes entered her vision. And the next she knew Dacre had placed warm, sensitive fingers beneath her chin. And was forcing her to look at him.

He said something about '*très adorable*', but, made to look at him, Josy couldn't miss seeing that the look in his eyes wasn't cool or distant as she had feared it might be. In those grey depths she could see nothing but warmth.

'You are well this morning?' he wanted to know.

Was he teasing? She couldn't decide. 'Quite well,' she replied.

'But you don't like me this morning?' he enquired, and Josy, hearing something in his voice—she wasn't sure what, but it was a tinge of something that suggested that it bothered him that she might not like him—could only speak the truth.

'I—um—think I've gone shy again,' she mumbled.

'You *are* adorable!' he smiled, and, his head coming nearer, their lips met.

She felt his arms come round her as he gathered her to him, and felt his body against her as he moved closer. 'Oh, Dacre!' she gasped as their kiss broke, and stared at him in confusion and amazement. For how could it be? Last night she had been a shy, unawakened virgin. And now, this morning, Dacre only had to touch her and she wanted him to make love to her!

'It's the same for you too?' he asked, and she marvelled again that he seemed to know exactly what she was feeling.

'You too?' she asked shyly.

'Have you no idea what you do to me?' he asked, keeping her in the circle of his arms, but with a smile answered for her, 'No, I don't suppose you have.' Lightly then he kissed her mouth. 'But,' he went on, 'we have important matters to deal with today, to discuss.' And, as if searching for more control, he decided promptly, 'I don't think, *ma petite*, that your bedroom, with your bed looking so inviting, is the place where we should discuss anything. We will go to the stables.' Not giving her time to think, he dragged his gaze away from the bed and hurried her from her room. Together they went down the stairs. 'Can you wait for breakfast?' he asked. 'I have something I want to show you.'

'Of course,' she murmured, loving him with all she had, and food of small importance.

She had thought that they would walk to the stables, but once outside the house she saw Dacre's car waiting there. Clearly to have got his car out of its garage must mean that he had already been out or intended to go out. He held the door for her and she got into the passenger seat, while she hid the sudden anguish she felt at the thought that perhaps Dacre meant to take a drive to the airfield. She didn't want him to leave—ever.

Josy tried to calm herself by making herself remember that Dacre had something he wanted to show her. It must be good if he wanted to show her in a hurry.

It did not take long to reach the stables, but before they got there Josy was deep into what else Dacre had said. He'd said, 'We have important matters to deal with today.' *We*, not him. She and him! She swallowed hard on a suddenly dry throat. Matters to discuss, he had said.

Her head was in a whirl when Dacre halted the car in the stableyard. 'Someone's turned Nina and César out,' she guessed when, leaving the car, she saw that their stalls were empty.

'They're in the paddock.'

'I'm sorry—I'm late this morning.'

'Understandably late this morning,' Dacre qualified, and remarked, causing her to go a trace of pink, 'You didn't get to sleep until the early hours.' He paused, seemed to hesitate, then, looking down at her, he quietly asked, 'Any regrets?'

She looked into his eyes, loved him dearly. He had made her feel like a woman. And no matter what happened today—even should the matters they had to deal with, to discuss, be matters related to her returning home—then never would she or could she regret a thing. She was suddenly feeling too choked to be able to speak, and all she was capable of doing just then was shaking her head.

But it was the answer that Dacre wanted, for, placing an arm about her shoulders, he held her to him for a moment. 'Come, let's go and see the horses in the paddock,' he suggested, and with his arm about her shoulders they walked from the stableyard and round the corner towards the paddock.

They were almost up to the paddock rail, however, when Josy stood stock-still. Dacre halted too. 'There are—three horses there,' she said slowly.

'Are you sure?' he questioned—but there was no mistaking the hint of teasing in his voice. Josy glanced to him, but then her glance went swiftly back to the paddock where the third horse—the stranger in the camp—had picked up the sounds of voices and had turned; and as the horse moved and started to trot over—with Nina and César following—a feeling of gladness entered her heart.

'Hetty!' Josy cried, and took off at a gallop herself. Oh, Dacre, she thought; this, then, was what he had wanted to show her. She met Hetty by the paddock rail and leaned over and hugged and kissed her—and had to pat Nina and César when they trotted over too before returning to Hetty to croon, 'How did you get here?'

Then, having never forgotten him, Josy became aware of Dacre standing right there with her. And it was he who replied, 'You remember the business I had to attend to last night?'

Keeping one hand on Hetty's neck, Josy turned to him. 'Hetty arrived last night?'

'The phone call I took was to say that Hetty and horsebox had made it as far as Angers,' he revealed, and added enchantingly, 'Before I could come to you, *ma petite*, I had to wait for the horsebox, and after that, having transferred her to a stable, wait to check that she had everything you would want her to have, and to stay with her a while to make sure she was happily settled.'

'Oh, Dacre,' she said softly, hardly able to believe that Hetty was here, that Dacre had brought her here—that he had done all that last night. Her hand slipped from the mare's neck, and as he fed the three horses a sugar lump each and they trotted back to the shade, Josy asked, 'But—why?'

'Why?' he returned, his expression deadly serious as he looked back at her. 'Why else, my dear, than because I wanted you to stay?'

'Stay?' she queried, stunned, her heartbeats starting to race.

Dacre glanced from her to the wooden seat where she had so often sat watching the horses. 'Let's go and sit down—I said we had important matters to deal with—to discuss.'

Josy went with him to the seat, her heart thumping. From the seriousness of his expression she had an idea that the 'matters' were indeed very important. Oh, heavens, she felt a bag of nerves, half fearing that Dacre would tell her that he wanted her to go, but pinning all her hopes on the fact that Hetty was there and that Dacre had definitely said that he wanted her to *stay*.

Once they were seated Dacre turned to her, and Josy, looking at him, wished he would smile. Though, since her own smile seemed to have gone into hiding from the sudden uproar of her emotions, she doubted if she would have been able to smile back at him.

'Y-you said you—brought Hetty over because...' she began when the feeling of tension in her became more than she could bear, only to have her voice fail on her.

'I knew you were missing her.' Dacre, to her relief, took over. But suddenly some of his solemnity faded as he confessed, 'I didn't want you to have any reason to return to England. Because, after all my efforts to get you here, you might go—and never come back.'

Josy was totally fascinated by this insight into the way his thoughts had gone. But while she stared—and her thoughts all over the place—she tried to look deeper into what he was saying, the best she could sort out was, 'Efforts?'

'Efforts,' Dacre agreed, and caught hold of her hand as he confided, 'Dear Josy, I have not always told you the truth, I'm afraid.'

'You lied to me?' She wasn't very sure how she felt about that.

'Believe me, trust me, *petite*; I regard you too highly to lie to you for any reason other than that which necessity forced on me.'

She couldn't begin to understand what he meant, but, at a moment when she might have pulled her hand from his, the fact that he'd stated he regarded her highly caused her to let it remain there.

'Have you done lying to me, do you think?' she asked, a trifle drily she had to own—and loved him when that brought a wry smile to his face.

'How you have changed this past year,' he commented.

'I've grown more confident since I've been here,' she admitted. And because it was his due added, 'And I thank you for that.'

'You think it's all my doing?' Clearly he doubted it.

'Since knowing you I've rediscovered I have a temper. That I can get angry—'

'I noticed that!' It was his turn to offer a dry note.

'Anyhow,' she went on quickly, suddenly realising only then that his having stirred her emotionally way back in England—albeit anger—could only have been the start of her falling in love with him. 'Um...' She didn't want him guessing at her love for him. 'Why did you find it necessary to lie to me?'

'Because I wanted you here with me,' he replied unhesitatingly.

'But—but... But you asked me to come here months and months ago. You asked when you came to England— the end of last September—if I would help you by coming to look after your horses. You said you lived in a very isolated—' She broke off when it looked as though Dacre wanted to interrupt. 'What?' she asked.

'I shall tell you no more lies, my dear; we have come too far for that!' he wasted no time in replying. And, while her heart started to race, added, 'But, to confess to some old—um—untruths, I must tell you that at the time of asking you to come and look after my horses— while stressing the isolation of my home because I judged that somewhere isolated would appeal to you—I did not then—um—own any horses.'

Josy stared at him in amazement. 'You didn't *own* any?' She gasped. 'But...' She was lost. 'Would you mind explaining?' she asked, adding quickly, since her brain didn't appear to be coping very well, 'From the very beginning.'

Dacre looked at her for long, long moments, and then told her quietly, 'I should like to.' First, though, he raised her dainty hand to his lips and kissed it, while Josy fought to keep calm—and failed miserably. 'It began, my little love, when I went to meet Marc and his bride at the airport in Nantes.'

'Then?' she queried, his endearment causing her heart to palpitate, which didn't help her confusion at all. Apart from during that drive from the airport to Marc's parents' home, and perhaps for half an hour afterwards, she hadn't seen Dacre again for almost four months.

'I met you, dear Josy—and didn't know what hit me,' he told her quietly, his eyes fixed on hers.

What was he saying? Whatever, it was doing nothing for her fast-beating heart. 'You—er—didn't?' she enquired huskily.

'I didn't,' he agreed. 'There you were so very shy, so very beautiful, so unaware of your own beauty—I at once fell totally in love with you.'

'Y—' Her voice caught in her throat, and not a peep more would come.

'I couldn't then believe it myself.' He smiled.

'You were—um—infatuated, perhaps?' she found enough voice to suggest.

'That was the best I could hope for. But I knew even then that—as at some future date I started lying to you— I would be lying to myself to try to deny my love.'

Dacre had loved her! She could hardly believe it was true. She wanted quite desperately to ask if he still loved her, but she didn't have the nerve. Though, as she remembered his tenderness, his understanding with her last night, a smile of beginning to believe started to shine in her.

'You wanted to deny it?' she asked huskily.

'*Chérie*, I had to! You were my cousin's bride, the ink on your wedding papers barely dry. There was I, a man who would never agree to love from afar, in love with someone who had just committed the rest of her life to my cousin—a cousin I loved like a brother. I couldn't take it. I felt as if everything I'd worked for and enjoyed all these years was crumbling about me.'

'Oh, Dacre,' she murmured softly, stunned still, but her feelings all for him.

He seemed to like the sound of his name on her lips, for he placed an arm firmly about her shoulders before going on, 'I was so stunned at this emotion creating havoc in me that when I delivered you and Marc to his parents I stayed but a short while and—my vacation plans for the next day suddenly having little appeal—I flew off that night in an opposite direction, to a little-known Greek island. I needed to get right away—needed to think, needed solitude—and hopefully I would realise I had made a mistake.'

'H-had you made a mistake?' she just had to ask.

His arm about her shoulders tightened. 'No, *mon ange*, I hadn't. It was, as I knew, irrevocably there—there in the fact that your beautiful face and manner haunted me the whole of the two weeks I was away.' Tenderly he kissed her brow. 'I returned from Greece to discover that both my father and my office had been urgently trying to contact me—and that Marc, killed riding that beast, was already buried.'

'I'm so sorry,' she stated softly, in her love for him all her sympathy going out to him for the shock that news must have been to him.

Only to find that Dacre, in his love for her, had been more concerned for her, when he revealed, 'I was still taking in Marc's death when I enquired about you. You were in deep shock, my aunt told me. And as I started to grow furious that they had allowed you to return to England on your own Aunt Sylvie told me how your fiercely protective twin had flown over and had escorted you back.'

'Belvia was marvellous.'

'I'm so glad you had her,' Dacre commented on a heartfelt note. 'I wanted to come to England to see you then myself,' he confessed. 'I should have done. As soon as you told me of the misapprehension you'd been under, the guilt that had riven you, I knew I had been mistaken not to come. I could have told you of that evil-hearted stallion—that it was Marc's love of him and not inattention because of the terror he put you through on your wedding night that caused his death.'

'I don't remember much of what went on around me in those early days except for the guilt,' Josy owned. But she found a smile as she added, 'Thanks to you, that dreadful guilt started to fade, and has now gone.'

'Oh, I'm so glad, *chérie*!' Dacre exclaimed. '*Je t'aime*,' he breathed, as if he could not help himself, and as Josy realised that Dacre had just told her in French 'I love you', she raised her head—and their eyes met. 'Oh, my sweet, sweet flower,' Dacre whispered, and kissed her a kiss of such beauty that when he pulled back she could only look at him. She knew indisputably then that he loved her. She wanted to tell him that she loved him—just how much she loved him—but wretched shyness seemed to glue the words to her throat. 'So, to explain

everything, my heart, to explain the extent of my lies—
since I am never, ever going to lie to you again—I must
tell you that while still emotionally shaken that we had
lost Marc, emotionally shaken at the fact that the love
I had for you seemed stronger at that dreadful time, I
began to feel hypocritical. I began to feel that my reasons
for wanting to go to England were more that I just had
to see you rather than that I felt I had to come and offer
you my condolences.' Josy stared at him and he went
on, 'For that same reason I denied the need to phone
or to write to you. But four months later I could deny
my need to see you no longer.'

'You were in England on business,' Josy recalled.

'A lie, *mon adorable*,' Dacre confessed. 'No matter
how I tried, I couldn't get you out of my head. I just
had to come and see you. To invent being in England
on some business seemed a good cover.'

'I'd no idea!' she gasped.

And gently he kissed her. 'My poor Josy, how sad,
how unhappy, how pale you looked. It was like a knife
twisting in my heart to see you so. I could not bear that
it was so. I wanted you in France, where I could take
care of you.' He smiled then as he stated, 'I knew from
Marc's parents of your love of horses. To invent having
a couple of horses that I needed someone reliable to look
after was the best, if slender, chance I could think of to
tempt you at that time.'

'But I fell for it.' She had to smile too.

'Not straight away. But I thought I'd seen a spark of
interest, and, for all you'd refused, my foolish heart
started to pound at the thought that if the gods were
kind there might be a hope that I would see you
every weekend.'

'Oh, Dacre,' she whispered. 'It was like that for you?'
Her heart was pounding too, right at that very moment,

as it began to sink in how very much he must have loved her—and still did.

'You cannot know, *mon coeur*,' he murmured, and kissed her gently before, as if he wanted it all said and out of the way, he pulled back and resumed, 'Purchasing a couple of horses, making a paddock and transforming some old outbuildings into stables was the easy part. The hard part was learning patience.'

'You're not normally a patient man?'

'Not then, my darling,' he replied. 'But I was fully aware of your shyness, and knew how carefully I must go with you if I didn't want to ruin everything. I'd been to the stables in England with you, and had become more and more enchanted by you when, your inhibitions falling from you, I observed a loving, tender side of you when you saw your Hetty. You asked if I would wait while you went for a ride on her—and I knew then, my dearest love, that I would wait for you for however long it took.'

'You've—been—wonderful,' she had to admit, even if, unused to speaking so, she spoke the words shyly.

'I'm glad you think so,' he grinned. 'I have to admit, *petite*, that hope and frustration in getting you here were warring enemies in my long wait for you. You took over six months to come to me!' he accused, and Josy burst out laughing.

'I'm glad I came,' she told him.

'No more than I,' he told her sincerely. 'I've so ached for you. You'll never know the joy in my heart that day when I could no longer resist the urge to hear your voice and I rang your home—and you told me you would like to take the job.'

'I'd no idea!' she exclaimed huskily.

'*Naturellement*.'

Josy smiled at him, loving him with all she had as she explained, 'I think I was starting to come to terms with Marc's death when you rang. I was still nursing a whole load of guilt, I know, but I was also starting to take stock, and realising that I must do something about making a different sort of life for myself. I'd just decided that I would go to France for six months, and make the break with my father, when, right at that moment, you rang.'

'And I was so euphoric after that phone call. I wasn't to know then that I was going to have to wait, and to wait, and wait some more for you to come.'

'My father was ill—'

'In view of your severely shocked state I should have written to him telling him I would take the greatest care of you—but I didn't for fear he might devise obstacles to your coming to me.'

'Was that how you felt—thought?' she gasped.

'It was,' he owned. 'Already there were too many delays in your coming to me.'

'You rang me Christmas Day!' she remembered.

'I had to. I was near to despair. Thank God I didn't know then that I'd have to wait until April to see you. But you, darling Josy, rang in February to give me a definite date when you'd be here, and I told you that Nina and César were looking forward to seeing you when in reality it was me that was eagerly looking forward to seeing you—and I thought I'd better do something about brushing up my rusty riding skills.'

'You don't normally ride?' she exclaimed, amazed.

'I hadn't ridden in years,' he confessed. 'For you I endured that—and more. And then that April day—when I'd been at the window most of the morning willing you to arrive—at three-thirteen that afternoon my straining ears heard the sound of your car. I waited a couple of minutes, deciding to be friendly but casual. And then I saw you, and all I knew was that, starved all those months for a sight of you, I had a desperate need to touch, to hold you.'

'You did—you held my arms and kissed my cheeks.'

'I was aware my action worried you when you stiffened as I held you. It endorsed for me that if ever I was to gain my heart's desire with you, I must find still more patience.' He smiled into her eyes. 'You have no idea how difficult that became when, with each new part I learned about you, I fell deeper and deeper in love with you.'

'You—did?' she asked chokily, her heart thundering; he did love her. He did, he did, he did!

'How could I help it? As shy as you are, you recognised shyness in my housekeeper, and I witnessed how you overcame your own shyness out of a sensitivity to put Agathe at her ease. Is it any wonder that I am enchanted? That I wanted to spend more and more time with you, to form a friendship, to build on that friendship, to gain your trust and—should good fortune be with me—perhaps gain a little of your love?'

'Oh, Dacre,' she sighed.

And he smiled tenderly, and told her, 'But, as reserved as you are, I've seen you angry and spirited. I've seen you with an imp of mischief dancing in your eyes and, with a speeding heart, I've known delight in seeing you emerge from the darkness that engulfed you. But, *mon petit ange*, when the love in my heart became too much to hold in I had to realise my weakness in being too impatient and deliberately force myself to stay away from you.'

'You've stayed away from your home because of me?' she exclaimed, astounded.

'It is true,' he admitted. 'I've had to pretend I've had a lunch engagement elsewhere when there has been none. Or that I had something to keep me in Paris at the weekend, or even to make me leave here for Paris earlier than I'd intended, when there was nothing in me but a desire to be with you.'

'I didn't know!' she gasped.

'I fear it would have terrified you if you had,' he commented softly. 'Don't you see, sweet flower, that I had to allow you to come to me in your own time? My problem was that I have always been intolerant of delay.'

'You've been through a very bad time,' she realised.

'So too have you, little one,' he murmured tenderly— and it seemed the most natural thing in the world that they should cleave to each other and kiss.

'Oh, my dear!' she whispered as their kiss broke and they pulled back to look into each other's dear face. 'Has it been so very dreadful?'

'There were better moments than the dread that took me that Saturday when I came looking for you on César and met a riderless Nina halfway. I have never been so panicked or, when I saw you lying there motionless, so terrified. I thought you might be dead.' He smiled then as he went on, 'Only you weren't dead, but shrieking loud enough to wake the dead when I dared to touch you.'

'I'm so sorry,' she apologised.

'So you should be,' he admonished teasingly. 'There am I, fearful that I have lost you before I've won you one minute, then the next, when my attention is merely to feel for your pulse, you are turning on me in panic and yet—while I don't like at all the fact that there is panic in your eyes at my touch—causing me to fall deeper in love with you than ever by showing me yet more of your spirited side—when you ride off without me.'

She had to smile, but confessed, 'I wanted to apologise. Back at the stables I cooled down and... But you came by and looked so aloof that I couldn't say a word. And then I had the dreadful feeling you wanted me to leave and—'

'Oh, sweet and wonderful Josy! To be aloof was all I could be. Otherwise I would have taken you in my arms.'

'Truly?' she exclaimed.

'Most truly. I had such a feeling of wanting to hold you—not sexually, *ma petite*. But, just as at other times I've felt a tremendous need to be near you, to sometimes stretch out a hand just to touch you, so it was then, when, still feeling shaken from imagining you injured or worse, I had to fight an urgent need to hold you.'

'Oh, I'm so sorry,' she apologised again, and Dacre placed a light kiss on the corner of her mouth.

'As for wanting you to leave, *chérie*—I had waited over six months for you to come to me; there was no chance I would let you go if I could help it.'

What could she do? She kissed him, and smiled at him as she confessed, 'If it's—er—of any—interest, I—er—well, the thing is, if I'm honest—'

'I want only honesty between us from now on, my own,' he put in quietly.

She gave him a warm smile and confessed, 'Well, to be honest, you were too disturbing to me.'

'Disturbing?'

'I think I was starting to be aware of you—um—in a way I had never been aware of a man before.'

'*Petite*!'

'Oh, I wasn't aware of what exactly was happening to me at the time. But now I think I can see that when last September you came to England, and you suggested I start riding again, and I definitely felt angry with you—

I think even back then I was aware of you as Dacre Banchereau rather than merely Marc's cousin.'

'Please, whatever you do, my flower, do not stop there,' he ordered.

Josy laughed, and as she began to appreciate how much Dacre loved her, how careful and controlled he had been in his love for her, so for him, she tossed away any remnants of shyness to tell him openly, 'You made me angry; you made me laugh. You even made me feel rebellious—something was very definitely getting to me about you. I even found myself telling you of matters that had been locked up in me since I was fifteen—things I'd never told another living soul!'

'I wondered about that,' he put in softly. 'Were you beginning to trust me in a way you had never trusted Marc; or was it that I was so unimportant to you that it didn't matter to you that you'd told me? Because of that, little one, I kept out of your way for most of the weekend—and even told myself I wouldn't come home the next weekend.'

'But you did,' she recalled.

'And felt most put out that you spent the whole time— or most of it—out with the horses,' he remembered too. 'Then, a couple of weeks later, I invited you to the Cadre Noir—and you, obviously enjoying your own company, arrogantly told me you'd already been.'

'Arrogantly?' she queried.

'I'm sensitive,' he grinned. 'I thought you'd been out with that damned vet!'

'You didn't! You were jealous?'

'As jealous as hell,' he agreed. 'Apart from the fact that Franck and Georges very soon grew to like the young widow from England very much, they also had instructions to watch over you like a favourite daughter when I wasn't here. So I was confident that no one would

worry you while you while you were on my property.'
And, smiling into her eyes, he murmured, 'So, having
overlooked the fact that there would be times when I'd
have to invite a vet here, I started to go quietly out of
my mind about him—about you—while at the same time
I was forced to acknowledge that the time for the—' he
broke off to search for the right word '—togetherness I
was trying to form with you was not yet right. I deliberately stayed in Paris the next weekend.'

'But you came home the following Friday,' she inserted quietly.

'I couldn't keep away. It was your wedding anniversary; I couldn't bear you to be unhappy and alone.'

'You came especially...?'

'Have you not realised yet how adored by me you are?'
he enquired simply.

'Oh, Dacre,' she cried weakly.

'You have suffered enough, little one,' he breathed,
and kissed her tenderly before he went on to tell her, a
humorous note entering his voice, 'And so have I. By
then I was loving you so much that I was having a con-
stant battle to hold it in. I was starting to feel a nervous
wreck, scared that at any moment I might break, give
in, and ruin all I was hoping to achieve by taking you
in my arms and telling you how I felt about you.'

He *had* been through hell, she realised. 'Was that why
you didn't come home the next weekend?' she asked.

Dacre nodded. 'Did you miss me?'

Shyness, which she despaired ever being free of,
threatened to swamp her again. But with Dacre being
so open with her she wanted with all she had to be as
open with him. 'Jealousy isn't purely your prerogative,'
she told him—and saw a smile break from him that was
wonderful to see.

'You thought I was nightclubbing in Paris with—!' he exclaimed, with a grin. 'And were you jealous?'

'When I wasn't anxious that you might be ill,' she admitted shyly, and was kissed for that admission, but, fearing another battle with shyness should he question her about her jealous feelings, she swiftly reminded him, 'You flew down from Paris on Wednesday.'

'I was desperate for the sight of you by then,' he owned. 'I just had to obey a compulsion to come and see you—only you weren't here when I arrived. Agathe said you were in Angers, so I came looking for you.'

'You had an errand in Angers,' she reminded him.

'You were my errand, *petite*. I came only to find you.'

'Oh—Dacre!' she laughed. 'And you did find me.'

'Oh, I did. I found you impudent, saucy, delightful—and felt more in love with you than ever. Is it any wonder, *chérie*, that when I follow you home and find my laughing companion at lunch has gone, I should lose my control in the frustration of the moment and blurt out that I want to marry you?'

'I... What can I say?' she asked helplessly.

'Your look of horror said it all for you,' he stated. 'And,' he confessed, 'it terrified me too—until our discussion that evening, when I learned of the terrible burden—terrible and unnecessary burden—you had been carrying alone.' He held her warmly to him. 'By last Sunday, my adorable Josy, I was having to rethink my strategy. I knew by then of your conviction that you were frigid. But, while Marc's unfortunate behaviour had petrified you and had not helped you at all to overcome your natural modesty, I thought it was probable that your belief you were frigid stemmed not only from Marc's behaviour but also from your own fear of violence. I was very much aware, little one, of the dense barriers to be negotiated.'

'You've thought about me a lot,' she realised.

'Constantly,' Dacre answered. 'You, my dear, were very much on my mind on Sunday as I lay in my bed having given up my attempt to read as I wondered if my new strategy of being more in your company in an endeavour to make you feel more comfortable with me was the right one. You hadn't wanted to spend a companionable evening with me in the *salon* after dinner.'

'I was a bit—er—mixed up,' she confessed. 'I think it was starting to dawn on me that I couldn't go on the way I was, that I had to show you—since you wouldn't take my word for it—that there was no future for us together as a married . . .' Her voice faded, but her heart rejoiced at the wonderful all-loving smile that he gave her.

'And what a brave way you chose to show me, my sweet Josy,' he murmured. 'You'll never know the pounding in my head, in my heart when you came into my room and asked, ' "Can I sleep with you?" '

'You thought me forward?'

'I thought you entirely enchanting. You had once said to me that being brave was doing something that terrified you, and I knew how brave and terrified you were.' His voice deepened emotionally. 'I also knew, sweetest love, that to come to me when you were so terrified, to be so brave, so courageous must surely have meant— and my heart, I confess, was bursting at the thought— that you cared for me.'

She smiled shyly, and could not deny it, and he gently touched her lips with his. 'And I also knew, as I invited you into my bed, that then, more than at any other time, I had to control my—um—masculine urges. I found that far easier,' he owned, 'when I felt your nerve-racked body shaking beneath my arm. All I wanted to do then was to ease that dreadful time for you.'

'You were thinking only of me—not yourself?'

'You are my life,' he breathed sincerely.

'Oh, what a lovely thing to say,' she sighed.

'It's true.' He kissed her.

'You said goodnight, and went to sleep,' she murmured dreamily.

'I said goodnight, but slept little,' he corrected her. 'I was fully awake at dawn when, like a rocket from a missile launcher, you shot out of bed and out of my room.'

She laughed; she had to—it was pretty much the way it had been. 'I couldn't believe in the cold light of day that I'd been so bold,' she confessed. 'And yet I came to your room a second time—and you were again kind,' she remembered.

'How else would I be, dear love? I was trying to get you used to me, used to small intimacies. I wanted you to feel less nervous of me. In short, I wanted you to trust me.'

Josy looked at him steadily. 'I think I did. I—in the morning I kissed you—'

'Without fear in your eyes,' Dacre inserted gently.

'You—expected fear when...?'

'Oh, yes. We were getting closer to each other. But on Tuesday night you didn't come to me, and I realised that the intimacy we'd so far achieved would be as nothing—that the chance to let you discover for yourself that you weren't frigid would be gone—unless I did something about it.'

'You came to my room. You said you couldn't sleep.'

'Nor did I sleep. I spent most of that night fighting, holding down the urge to kiss you awake.'

'I didn't know...'

'I went back to my own room before dawn. Then last night at dinner you said you would miss me a little next week when I returned to Paris, and I was sure it must mean that you cared a little for me. For my part, although I'm already busy rearranging my work schedule so that I can do more work here, I shall not be able to leave at all unless you come with me.' Her heart, which had been cantering and galloping in turns, picked up speed again to hear him intimate that he intended to spend more time in his country home but that when he returned to Paris he wanted her with him! 'I knew then, last night at dinner, that we—you and I—had reached a point of no return.'

'You—um—wanted to stay with me last night, you said.'

'And you said you were scared, and I couldn't tell you, precious darling, that I was scared too—because if it all went wrong I stood to lose you for ever.'

'Oh, Dacre.' She smiled lovingly at him, and trusted him so much that she just didn't mind at all if he'd guessed that she thought him something pretty special.

'You're lovely,' he breathed, and held her close up against him for long, loving moments. 'And I love you so very much,' he added huskily. 'Can you not now, my shy darling, tell me of your feelings for me?'

Josy was by then fairly certain that he must know of her feelings for him. But love, as she had realised, was a jittery taskmaster. So she gathered every scrap of courage and began, 'You asked me that day when we came back here after lunching in Angers what was wrong. I couldn't tell you then, but that day, in that café, when I looked up and saw you there so unexpectedly—well, that was when I knew that I—um—cared very much for you—' She broke off to swallow, and felt his arm about her tighten, felt the tenderness of his kiss to the side of her face.

'Go on, *petite*,' he urged, and, as if he knew that there was more, he bade her, 'Don't stop there.'

'Well, I was so happy then. But...'

'But?'

'I was on my way home when cold common sense doused me in icy water. What was the point in caring? Nothing was ever going to come of it. And then you were there, asking what was wrong—and horrifying me by saying you wanted me to marry you.'

'And now?' Dacre asked very quietly.

'Now?' She wasn't with him.

'Now you know that something *can* come of it—what now?' he asked, a kind of tension in him as he waited for her answer.

Oh, heavens, she loved him so. Josy took a deep, shyness-banishing breath.

There had been a few occasions in her life when some quality which she had little control over had reared up out of her frustration with her inadequacies and pushed her headlong through those stout bastions of reserve. Such an occasion happened then when, loving Dacre with her whole heart, she took a deep breath and answered, 'And now, I think, if it's all right with you, that I'd like very much—to marry you.'

'*Chérie*. My Josy! I adore you!' he cried. And, exultant, he added, 'I knew! Last night I knew you loved me! You do love me, don't you?' he demanded, his grey eyes burning fiercely into hers.

'Oh, yes,' she replied, quite unable to believe the utter joy on his face. 'I love you so much.'

He gave another cry of rejoicing. 'And you'll marry me?' he insisted, as if he couldn't believe his hearing when she had said that to marry him was what she would like to do.

'Oh, yes,' she whispered.

And Dacre heard, and, standing up, taking her with him, he embraced her in his arms. 'One kiss, maybe two,' he decreed, 'Then we must go and arrange a wedding.'

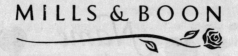

MILLS & BOON

Next Month's Romances

Each month you can choose from a wide variety of romance with Mills & Boon. Below are the new titles to look out for next month.

LAST STOP MARRIAGE	Emma Darcy
RELATIVE SINS	Anne Mather
HUSBAND MATERIAL	Emma Goldrick
A FAULKNER POSSESSION	Margaret Way
UNTAMED LOVER	Sharon Kendrick
A SIMPLE TEXAS WEDDING	Ruth Jean Dale
THE COLORADO COUNTESS	Stephanie Howard
A NIGHT TO REMEMBER	Anne Weale
TO TAME A PROUD HEART	Cathy Williams
SEDUCED BY THE ENEMY	Kathryn Ross
PERFECT CHANCE	Amanda Carpenter
CONFLICT OF HEARTS	Liz Fielding
A PAST TO DENY	Kate Proctor
NO OBJECTIONS	Kate Denton
HEADING FOR TROUBLE!	Linda Miles
WHITE MIDNIGHT	Kathleen O'Brien

Name that Song

How would you like to win a year's supply of simply irresistible romances? Well, you can and they're free! Simply solve the puzzle below and send your completed entry to us by 31st October 1996. The first five correct entries picked after the closing date will each win a years supply of Temptation novels (four books every month—worth over £100).

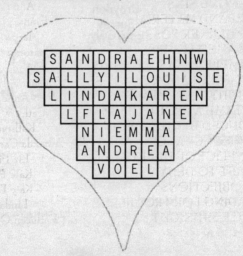

S	A	N	D	R	A	E	H	N	W
S	A	L	L	Y	I	L	O	U	I	S	E
L	I	N	D	A	K	A	R	E	N
	L	F	L	A	J	A	N	E
	N	I	E	M	M	A
	A	N	D	R	E	A
	V	O	E	L

Please turn over for details of how to enter ☞

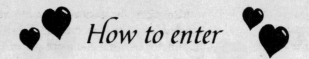 *How to enter*

To solve our puzzle...first circle eight well known girls names hidden in the grid. Then unscramble the remaining letters to reveal the title of a well-known song (five words).

When you have written the song title in the space provided below, don't forget to fill in your name and address, pop this page into an envelope (you don't need a stamp) and post it today! Hurry—competition ends 31st October 1996.

**Mills & Boon Song Puzzle
FREEPOST
Croydon
Surrey
CR9 3WZ**

Song Title: _____

Are you a Reader Service Subscriber?   Yes ❑   No ❑

Ms/Mrs/Miss/Mr _____

Address _____

_____

_____ Postcode _____

One application per household.

You may be mailed with other offers from other reputable companies as a result of this application. If you would prefer not to receive such offers, please tick box. ❑

C396
D